THE FORGOTTEN ONES

STANLEY GARLAND JR.

ISBN: 978-1-7358394-2-4

Verses used in the story are the New International Version Translation of the Bible.

Table of Contents

Chapter 1

June 1st, 2015

Outbreak – Aegis City

0800

Dr. Mark Simpson pulled at his collar while he looked around the conference room table. The sound of one of the other workers prattling on about something that didn't mean much to him at the moment was becoming simply white noise to his ears as his brain turned over the problem he currently faced. None of it mattered anymore. *All I have to do is get it outside and I can die peacefully*, he thought, releasing a deep sigh before recollecting himself.

Dr. Simpson wasn't particularly tall but he had a long neck. It made him feel taller than most. His intellect made women want him more than anything. His genius made him one of the best scientists in Aegis City. Some say he was a solid five on some days, and six when wearing a suit. But then again, the standard for what was good looking is widely debated in the scientific community.

"Are you okay, Mark?" A woman asked, nibbling her lower lip, eyes slightly wide, looking concerned from across the conference room table. In fact, Mark could feel many eyes on him from around the room. Perhaps he had missed something?

"It's nothing," Mark replied, lifting a hand to massage his temple with two fingers. He tilted his head forward, the stress and exhaustion weighing him physically down. Mark pulled out his handkerchief before wiping his forehead. *It's okay you can do this, Mark.*

The woman visibly relaxed and smiled before looking back down at her documents. The meeting resumed, giving him some space.

"Dr. Simpson," a loud, deep voice called from the other room. A large man in a fancy striped suit entered, looking around. His hair was slicked back sharply. He walked in shoulders back and strode towards Mark with purpose in his steps. "Dr. Simpson," he muttered again before scratching his chin.

Mark mentally jolted back to the present, lifting his head he looked around. He was quickly drawn back into his dark thoughts. Staring at the plain white board room wall where there was a beautiful painting of the Oak River Bay. He thought of his wife, Sheila, and how he proposed to her ten years ago. *I'm looking forward to some of that pizza with sausage on the other side of this.* He imagined the savory meal that awaited him.

"Dr. Simpson, are you okay?" the fancy suited man inquired again, frowning at Mark's inattentiveness.

Mark narrowed his eyebrows, *This man is unfit to lead.* Mark picked up and twirled his pen, finally turning to look at his director. "Yes, Sir," Mark managed to force out as naturally as possible; a slight smile on his face.

"How are the tests going for the new vaccine?" The director asked, arms crossed.

Mark never liked the new director. The man was a quack and retired doctor from the military. As far as Mark was concerned, the man knew nothing about medicine. He only knew how to stroke his own ego. "We are finalizing testing this morning and it will be ready to ship out later today," Mark replied, trying to answer swiftly so the director could go off and bother someone else.

"Brilliant," the director laughed obnoxiously. "Brilliantly done." He took his hand and roughly padded Mark twice on the shoulder.

Mark wanted to punch the director in the belly. He clenched his fist tightly, holding his emotions in check by a thread. *Behave, behave*, he thought the mantra in the back of his brain. There were greater things at stake.

"If there's nothing else, everyone is dismissed," the director stated, ending the meeting that Mark hadn't really heard a word of.

Mark stood, looking across the table at Amanda Wilson. Her long blonde pigtails and petite frame always brightened his day. She was tall, somewhat imposing to others. She was five foot ten and had a beautiful face. She distracted many members of her team with her beauty.

Mark didn't want her to get caught up in what was happening. *How do I protect her?* Mark ran his hands through what was left of his gray crew cut trying to brush away his anxious thoughts…

"You looked flustered," Amanda said as she was walking up to Mark with a gentle smile.

Mark tried to give a genuine smile but felt it stop before it graced his cheek bones. "Walk with me, Amanda." Mark turned around, walking briskly down the hallway toward the break room not waiting to see if she came or not, only trusting.

Not expecting the abrupt departure, it took Amanda a moment to comprehend his words and actions. She took several hurried steps trying to catch up. Her high heels hindering her quick movements. "You almost left me behind!" Amanda accused when she caught up, clutching her papers to her chest.

Mark knew that today was her favorite day of the week: Tuesday. She didn't have a particular reason why, but it felt better than Monday and that's the story she went with.

Mark looked at Amanda who was wearing her favorite brown collared shirt tucked into her denim long skirt with brown boots. "You look nice today," Mark said.

Amanda tilted her head at him a bit puzzled. "Thank you…" she trailed, he was acting oddly. "But...You seem to be awfully tired or stressed. What's up?"

Mark leaned in, whispering, "You should get out of town quickly."

"Why?" Amanda asked her eyebrow raising in inquiry as her mind turned over the meaning of the words he had uttered. As it started to potentially click her hand marginally tightening against the papers that rested against her. Her blood raced, eyes widening at the strange abrupt words. "You're scaring me, Mark." Glancing around nervously she hissed. What was he warning her about?

"I don't have time to explain," Mark stated softly, his voice serious and stern. A hint of urgency twinging the edges of his whispered words. Trembling he put his hands on her shoulders "Take this and get out of town." Mark shifted moving his left hand closer to Amanda's lab coat pocket and slipped something into it. "Read the letter later. Please go!" He hissed, glancing over his own shoulder.

Amanda stepped back in shock. "Are you serious? What's going on?" Her mind was still whirling with possibilities. What kind of trouble was he into? If this was a bad joke…. She felt the weight of the object in her pocket shift with her movement. But what had he given her? Reaching into her pocket, feeling a glass vial of sorts. Amanda's eyes widened, "I trust you, Mark. We've worked together for years." She let out a breath and licked her lips a bit nervously. This was real! She continued as calmly as she could force herself to be, "This is such an important day. We cured the Piken Virus but now you want me to leave?"

Mark thought back to the first child he saw with the virus. The child's eye exploded an hour after contracting it. *That poor child. Those terrorists put a pod in children's cereal so when they opened it… the chemical released onto them.* Mark looked at Amanda, his eyes dripping tears. He couldn't bring himself to speak, he was trying to compose his emotions, he couldn't look upset….he couldn't let on.

Amanda watched his features and noted the moisture in Mark's eyes..."If you would ask me to leave on such a significant day, then it must be important," She said, looking down at the ground.

Mark didn't say a word as his eyes fell on a picture on the break room wall of his team holding a plaque from the mayor for the significant breakthrough. They were supposed to meet the president in three weeks. Mark mentally shaking himself out of his retrieve forced out, "Get going and say I let you off because of all your hard work. They shouldn't question it." He signalled her with a wave of his hand for her to leave immediately. His eyes were still glued to the plaque. When he didn't hear her move, he turned to look at her, eyes still tearing up as his nose started to fill with mucus from his distress, "Go now!" he sharply growled, being sure to keep his voice low despite it cracking at the end. He'd never see her again… but maybe, maybe she'd get out alive.

Amanda froze, stealing herself she gave Mark a hug. "Whatever you're caught up in, be safe. I can't do much for you, but I trust what you say. Call me and let me know you're okay."

Mark nodded, letting a small smile finally hit his lips. Mark watched as Amanda left the break room heading towards the exit of the training wing. Mark leaned back heavily on the wall of the breakroom sighing and massaging his temple. She was heading out. He could at least save her. Forcing his eyes clear of moisture and taking a few deep breaths he went to head back to his workspace. He had to keep up appearances.

Step, step, step. He focused on each step, watching his feet as he moved. Each Step felt heavy, it was a chore to take it, but he had to keep moving. Go through the motions and then find a place to quietly die alone, out of sight and quietly… yes that was it. Step, step ,step. He struggled to lift his hand to turn the knob to his workspace but then numbly fell into mechanical actions. This was easier. Don't think, don't care, do as always-

"SURPRISE!!!" Mark walked into the room to a round of applause and a sea of faces he didn't have the mental power to recognize.

A man approached him before shaking his hand. "It's an honor to meet you, doctor."

Mark felt nauseous as another man came and guided him toward the table lined with breakfast platters. *How could they celebrate? If he knew his time was drawing near…After what I did!* Mark didn't feel practically hungry but maybe some food would help his nerves. He went to the aisle grabbing some pancakes and bacon.

My wife makes the best bacon. Mark went to look for a place to sit down. He saw a man with peculiarly fascinating glasses and a finely dressed woman. His mind was so numb. Mark couldn't tell if he really knew them or not nor did he particularly care right now.

"Hello everyone, how are you doing?" Mark smiled trying to glance at both individuals as normal as possible.

"We are well," the man said, returning the smile before turning his eyes back to the woman he was with.

Mark went to walk past them to an available table. As he passed the pair he felt something sharp graze his thigh. Mark winced and shifted his leg to look. *How did they get in so quickly?* Turning with fear in his eyes they landed back on the couple that was rising from their seats.

"Don't forget," the man said, putting his hands together, smiling a crooked grin before he put his hand on the small of the lady's back and walked off. They disappeared into the crowd easily.

"I wouldn't," Mark said to the space where they had been. How could he forget, it was all he could think about.

Mark looked at his watch. It was half an hour past 10 AM. He couldn't leave so soon. Mechanically Mark talked with many different women and men for what seemed like forever. He felt his stomach churn. "I must be going," Mark excused himself.

Slowly standing up, Mark dragged himself as naturally as he could muster to deposit his plate in the trash. He placed his hand over his belly, rubbing it. His stomach hurt… *I* — Mark raced out the door and into the hallway bathroom. Where he flung himself into the stall just in time as the breakfast poured out from his mouth into the waiting toilet below. *So much for breakfast.*

Mark wiped his mouth before pulling out a large clear bottle from his pocket. Mark looked down at his watch as it was fifteen minutes until 11AM. *Okay. Let's go. I can finally leave…*

Mark was immediately met with another man right after he left the bathroom. "Congratulations, Dr. Simpson!" the man said in a nasally high pitched voice that was reminiscent of nails on a chalkboard, sticking out his hand all smiles.

Mark took it, shaking and smiling largely though his mind was raw and mechanical. No emotion triggered in his mind. He had to go a bit further so he could get out. He nodded, and continued towards his goal. Step, step, step.

"You are the man, Dr. Simpson," another woman with short pigtails and freckles said, patting him on the back.

Step, step, step. Mark rounded the corner towards the main connection of their facility. The front door came into view as he saw all the people clapping all around him. The world felt as if it was frozen in time as Mark slowly paced toward the revolving glass doors of his paradise.

The warmth of the sun hit his face as he looked up, closing his eyes for a brief moment. He felt a rumble in his top right coat pocket. *I guess I have to face the music.*

Mark pulled out the phone as his worst fears materialized. His eyes traced the text and the picture attached.

+1(702) 997-3418

YOU DIDN'T THINK WE WOULD LET THEM GO DID YOU? The text message threatened.

Mark saw his wife and daughter riddled with bullet holes, strapped to their kitchen chairs, it was a bloody mess.

Damn it! Damn it! Baby girl my sweetie….oh my God… His hand trembled. Bile rose in his throat, he wanted to throw up what little was still in his stomach. His head was spinning, as tears pricked the corners of his eyes once more.

The phone rumbled again. He forced himself to look clenching his teeth so hard it made his jaw ache.

+1(702) 997-3418

FINISH THE JOB.

Mark clenched his fist to stop his trembling, looking at the sky. *God, I can't do it! I won't! With what little dignity I have left I will die before I do this. I have nothing else left to lose!*

A swift sharp sensation passed through him as a bullet lodged in the wall of the building beside him.

Mark turned to the right and felt a warm sensation on the left side of his body. He stumbled to the right as he leaned against the wall. *Oh no!*

Mark tried to cover his mouth, but it was too late. A strange sensation filled his nostrils.

"Oh my God!" A woman screamed before she ran up to him. "Are you okay?"

"What happened?" another man asked.

Mark felt the right side of his body as blood poured from his mouth.

"Please…." Mark muttered, gurgling. "Stay back."

Mark tried to cover his mouth, but he sneezed right into the woman's face.

"You have to go now and leave the city. Mark weezed out more blood spattering from the effort it took to speak. His strength leaving him, Mark fell roughly to the ground in a pool of his own blood. The cell phone with that damned message on it slipped from his nearly unconscious hand.

The woman sneezed. Her right arm was twitching violently. "What did you do to me?!" she screamed in terror. The woman scratched her face repeatedly, it was so itchy, so itchy! She had to make it stop. She couldn't help it! She scratched more vigorously as she started to leave rivers of blood where her nails pierced and dragged skin. She was panicking as she started to trash her head from side to side. When it felt like her neck turned sharply to the right with a pop as if handled by a chiropractor.

Mark laid motionless on the ground, laying in a crimson red pool of his blood. *I guess this is goodbye. Natalie, my sweet wife….Claudia my daughter… I will see you on the other side…* He could vaguely hear screaming around him, but his ears were starting to feel as if they were filled with cotton. It all was starting to seem so distant.

The woman fell to the ground, screaming as her eyes turned a clear white.

"What's wrong?!" a man said, running up to her in panic.

The woman rigidly stood with her back to the man. It seemed like her movements were jerky and lacked a fluid motion. She then slowly, lurching, turned around, her face bleeding and her nose slit open blood raining from the wounds on her face.

"What the hell!" The man's eyes glanced around as he turned around trying to run away as terror gripped him.

The woman lunged at him quickly, tackling him to the ground. She sank her teeth into his flesh ripping in his neck.

Goodbye, my sweet Natalie…. Mark's eyes closed for the final time. To the tune of screams and chaos being birthed.

Chapter 2

June 1st, 2015

Aegis City – 34th Street Downtown

0800

"Augh" A man with a short afro and dark skin rolled over in bed. *Is it already time to wake up?* Rubbing his eyes he slowly rolled to the left side of the bed.

The African American man stood, looking around his room. His eyes landed on the degree on the wall. *I still can't believe I finished my degree in less time than I thought.*

The plaque read: *DAREN CEDRIC SMALLS BACHELOR'S IN MINISTRY FROM THE UNIVERSITY OF AEGIS.*

Tucked slightly behind the frame was a card he was given. Each graduate had received a card with a random bible verse on it at graduation. His card read, *The Lord is close to the brokenhearted and saves those who are crushed in spirit.* The verse was Psalms 34:18. It made sense as to why he got that verse. The downtown area where he lived many of the people were broken-hearted and he was commissioned to save them in the spirit.

Yawning, Daren stretched and cricked his neck to the side trying to get the blood flowing. "I spent too much time playing video games last night," he muttered to himself. Daren let out another yawn and crossed the small studio apartment to his television set. *I guess I should see what's on the news today.* Daren grabbed the remote of the TV off of his simple coffee table. Clicking the power on, Daren started flipping through the channels looking for reliable news.

"I guess Channel Five will do," Daren groaned, scratching his chin after he sat down on his soft sofa. He sighed delighted as the cushion enveloped him as he settled down. "This is ACN; Aegis City News with the latest report," the newscaster said with a big grin on his face. "The weather today will be a sunny ninety-two point three degrees with a 18% chance of rain."

"Not too bad," He muttered, mentally wincing at the idea of ninety degree weather. Running a hand through the fro, he sighed, "Some rain would be nice. It's been a hot drought all summer."

Getting up, he walked over to his blackout curtains and opened them. The summer sun shone brightly through the blinds. *Thank you, God, for another day to be alive. I need to lay off the video games though.*

Walking gingerly, Daren went to the restroom. He splashed some water on his face and cleaned it with a dark gray towel. He then stepped out to his kitchen area. Everything was in its place. The soft brown colors made for a soothing atmosphere not only for daily living but for romantic dates as well.

"Man, I am beat!" Daren shuffled to the counter, pulling out a large coffee cup and his favorite vanilla bean coffee from one of the cupboards. "Ahhh Richardson Brewing Company makes the best coffee." He muttered to himself as the coffee pot did it's magic. Soon the air was filled with the robust scent of coffee. Grabbing a cup and tossing in his essentials, creamer, sugar, and pumpkin spice mix he brought the black gold back with him to the sofa.

Daren had barely sat down on his lush brown sofa when he heard a knock at the door.

“Hey Daren, you up dawg! It’s your favorite cousin,” a man called loudly.

Oh, it's a bit too early for all of this, Daren thought to himself. “Coming,” Daren said, muting the tv and then standing back up to walk towards the door.

Peeping through the eye hole, he saw his cousin grinning from ear to ear. Daren opened the door. Immediately, he felt the tight embrace of the large muscular man.

“I’m proud of you, dawg!” his cousin said, squeezing him tighter. “Look at you finishing college and—”

“Could you let me go, Michael? You're crushing me!” Daren said, trying to eke out of the massive hug.

“Yo, I’m sorry cousin.” Michael stepped back sheepishly, picking up a plastic shopping bag on the ground.

Daren heaved a heavy sigh of relief, leaning over curiously trying to see the contents of the bag.

“You know what this is, Daren?” Michael grinned and held up the bag so the logo of the shop faced his cousin. “Let’s get this in!” Michael brought the bag in front of him, opening a box and revealing his favorite doughnuts.

Despite his large frame, Michael had a high pitch voice like a weasel. This led him to get picked on a lot in high school until he bulked up. *I always hated his voice.* Daren brought Michael in. *But he's one of the few cousins that checks up on me.*

"It's a shame your pops and mama couldn't be here to see you," Michael said, taking a bite of the vanilla sprinkled doughnut.

"Mom and Dad…" Daren said, looking down at his pumpkin spice coffee. It hurt to think about them…how long had it been since he lost them? Taking a moment to inhale the aroma of his morning drink, his thumbs playing along the rim of the cup in thought… two years now. It was two years ago that- his thoughts cut off.

"You know it's a bit weird to put pumpkin spice in your coffee in the summer. That's weird dawg." Michael made a face sticking his tongue out for emphasis. As he eyed his cousin critically.

Daren looked up from his drink and thoughts, trying to laugh.

"You know I'm trying to cheer you up, man." Michael was looking at him, there was a slight slump to his shoulders as the large man's eyes started to tear up though he didn't let the moisture fall. "Your mom and dad… "he trailed, bringing an arm up to wipe at his eyes quickly. Sniffing a bit he let out a breath and continued "they were like parents to me." His dark eyes still shiny from the moisture that was recollecting there locked with Daren's that were gathering their own tears. "I will always watch over you though. It's a shame they were killed…. like that… you know… the… the bombing…." He fumbled through the words not sure how much to end that sentence with. The feelings were still there of loss and pain.

Daren sighed, covering his own emotions by sipping his coffee before taking a bite from the sugar doughnut. He couldn't talk right now, or else he might crack. The mall bombing…if his parents hadn't gone that exact day then maybe they'd…he couldn't finish that thought.

Michael watched Daren carefully, measuring his movements. He quickly shifted to a more positive note with a smile and a sweep of his hand. "You know they are proud of you, dawg. You are the first person in the family to finish a degree. Crossing over to where his friend and cousin was sitting he sat next to him to look Darin directly in the eye, pointing at him. "The next generation will be looking up to you, man!"

"You are too kind, cousin," Daren smiled thinking about his parents.

He leaned back on the sofa looking up into the ceiling. He remembered his mom and dad. His father had greasy hair slicked to the side and Mom with her long black hair all natural. *Man. I miss them, God.*

"They're cheering on you, dawg," Michael leaned back. "I have a question for you cous'."

Daren looked up with a smile, not knowing what to expect. "Go ahead and shoot, Michael. "

Michael learned in conspiritively and whispered, "You got anything else other than vanilla coffee? You know I hate this wacky flavor."

"Sure." Daren laughed, pointing toward the cabinet. "Man, you're crazy. Why you hating on my coffee?" He demanded playfully.

Standing back up, Michael went to go where Daren had directed. "That vanilla coffee is weak sauce, man." He looked back at Daren grinning. "You know it's all about that dark roast, my friend."

Michael opened the new dark roast, smelling the grounds as he filled up the canister with water.

"I didn't forget, man." Daren said in a cheerful tone.

Daren looked at Michael's long dreadlocks. *He's never changed his hair style after all these years. I guess he keeps his circle of friends small. Not everyone will accept him the way he is.*

Daren's nostrils sniffed the vanilla aroma dissipate from the room as the cutting smell of dark roast filled the apartment. *So long, my sweet vanilla queen.*

Daren drew his favorite mug closer to his nose trying to drown out the overpowering smell of dark roast coffee.

"Anyway, man. When you going to move out of the hood?" Michael asked happily, watching as the coffee started to fill the pot. "You cash flowed your degree. It's time you reward yourself. You made this place nice despite the horrible area you live in."

"The landlord didn't mind me painting and making it my own. He's pretty chill."

Michael heard the coffee pot ding. "Ah perfection!" Michael said, pulling out a mug from the cabinet.

"You're drinking that black again, man?" Daren looked over at his cousin with a puzzled look.

"Yep. You know it's no creamer cousin. I like it black like I like women. Dark and smooth," Michael said, pouring the dark coffee into a medium sized mug.

Daren let out a slight chuckle.

"You know, "Michael started as he walked back over, "I got a room at my place. My girl moved out." He started conversationally.

"I'm sorry to hear that, cousin." Daren looked at him, his eyes glancing across to his cousin as Michael took his seat once more.

"It's all good, dawg." He chipperly replied smacking his knee before taking a sip, "She wasn't good for me anyway. I caught her cheating on me with some dude who doesn't even have a job. I almost busted a wine bottle over his square head. I feel like I have to clean out my apartment."

"Maybe that would have rounded it out," Daren said, laughing loudly at the idea of rounding the square headed interloper playing in his head.

"Psssspph" Michael swallowed carefully,before laughing himself, "You almost made me spew out my coffee. You stupid, Daren. I love ya cousin," Michael replied, trying to calm down his laughter. Taking a breath he put a hand on Daren's shoulder, "Real talk, dawg. Why not consider moving in? I don't like you living in a dangerous place like this. Shootings happen every week. What if you caught one of those bullets? I would really have to hurt someone and lose my job."

Daren shook his head, "I don't plan on becoming a bullet sponge, Michael. Plus the first time someone messed with me I gave them a mean right. Remember those boxing lessons we took back in high school?"

"Yeah. With coach Dominic. That was a mean brother," Michael said, laughing hard.

"He was but he instilled discipline in both of us which is why we are doing well while some of the other families are still struggling," Daren said in a melancholy tone.

"We have to set the example right," Michael said, raising his coffee cup. "Think about it. I need someone to cheer me up a bit."

"It's not like you to show too much negativity, Michael." Daren leaned forward, looking straight at his eyes, fixed on Michael's disposition.

"I'm good, cousin. I don't mean to worry you. You know I haven't seen you in a year. I've been busy trying to be like you. I started my associate degree in business so with that my job life is picking up."

"I'm proud of you too, dawg," Daren said smiling.

Michael looked at the coffee and back at his cousin, time to get back to the point, "Real talk, man. Why did you move to the hood? You could have moved in with me before I met that crazy woman."

"You already know, Michael." Daren took another sip of his coffee.

"Cousin, I get it. Those who need the gospel the most are in the inner city. Since you are training to become a minister...you want to be in the thick of the action. Who is going to love the least of these, right?"

"You got it, Michael," Daren replied. "Even though I could have lived somewhere nicer I've got to be the light."

"I admire you, cousin. Keep doing you. That hard work is going to pay off." Michael looked at the morning sun rising through the window. He wasn't going to convince him to move in this time either…well it had been worth a shot.

Michael and Daren reminisced on their childhood and the memories of Daren's parents.

"Look at the time, man." Michael looked down at his watch as it showed 11AM.

"What do you have going on?" Daren asked.

"I have this delivery I need to get too. My gym bag is in the car, I wanted to maximize my time with you." Michael smiled at Daren.

"I appreciate you." Daren leaned in his eyes pleading for an answer.

"I got this delivery I got to make. I'm not supposed to talk about it. Michael rubbed his fingers together. It's high profile but I am getting paid triple the amount. They want me to carry a strap as well. I feel more like a bank security guard instead of what I do."

"Maybe you are a security guard. You were in the service after all." Daren nodded slowly.

"Maybe I am," Michael said, letting out a hearty laugh. "Let me get going."

The two stood, giving each other a light embrace.

"Be good, man," Michael said, leaving a smile after his hug.

Daren watched Michael's long dreadlocks disappear out his door. *What a guy!* He thought. *I need to try to smile more.*

Daren walked back to the couch, lying down on the pillow before closing his eyes for a quick nap.

He fell into a deep sleep before a loud bang woke him up.

"Wha— What?" he muttered.

Daren grabbed his phone, it was 12:30 PM. He peered at the television hitting the mute button to turn the sound back on.

"What in the—"

Daren heard a faint alarm in the distance while gunshots rang throughout the neighborhood. *Those are semi auto shots.*

Daren's eyes widened, looking at the scene on his television.

"This is Aegis City Television," the women spoke in a somber tone. "The mayor has declared a state of emergency. The people—the people here are killing others. It's horrible. We are trapped on the roof of the main station. God help us all. Communications are starting to fail. Please stay safe. Accidents are blocking most major roads to the interstate. Please be safe. Oh God they're here! Keep filming!"

Daren covered his mouth as he watched in horror as deranged, crazed, and rabid people busted through the door, running toward the news crew.

"It's been a pleasure serving you," the woman shrieked, running to the edge of the roof.

Without a second to think, she jumped down to her death.

Daren immediately had a worried thought in mind. His cousin, Michael. He quickly grabbed his phone and dialed his number.

THE NUMBER YOU HAVE CALLED IS UNAVAILABLE.

Fear has gripped Daren's throat like a strangling barbed wire. *Oh God, please. Keep my cousin safe.*

Chapter 3

June 1st, 2015

Aegis City – 31st Street Downtown

0800

A young woman yawns before wincing with a hiss. Light streamed through her bedroom window. Reaching for her alarm clock, she brought her hand back and gingerly felt her bruised cheek with another hiss— which still stung from yesterday's incident.

The women in this city can be a bit harsh. Who knew sharing the gospel would be so cruel? It's nothing like the cities in Millington. She rubbed off the morning residue from her eyes.

The woman felt her phone buzz twice. She lifted her right hand and taped the bed a few times as she fumbled around without looking for the elusive phone. Finding it on the third try, the woman opened her flip phone looking down at the text.

Mom and Dad

+380 341-844-5580

Eline, it's your Mom. Remember to pray always and thank you for your courage. Going to another city across the ocean to minister is tough. No one wanted the assignment, but you took it. It was one of the worst cities you could go to. God will reward you for your servantship to him and kindness towards his creation. Your Papa says hi and looks forward to hearing from you soon. He has a job now and with your service we are receiving rations as well. Be kind to yourself and trust God. Let Jesus guide you. We love you.

Eline wiped her eyes looking down at her phone. *The church issued me this phone because we were too poor to afford it.*

Eline thought back to her town of Millington. It was a small mining town that was hit by a depression in 2013. The people there are hard but kind. The mayor had to make the difficult decision to exile certain families because of the employment drought. Too many needy people. The church has too much power there but without them most of the people would have starved to death. *I took up the mission of traveling across the ocean to minister and intern with the church here. In doing so it saved my family and they were able to keep their home.*

Eline rolled off the bed, and dragged herself to her closest, pulling out a semi long blue dress with black leggings. Her favorite flats sat in the small closet next to the bathroom.

"These will do!" she said excitedly. Immediately frowning at the pain in her cheek.

Eline stood at five foot six with brunette pigtails that went down to the small of her back. It was customary for a woman to grow long hair in her culture.

Walking over to the bathroom, she turned on the shower, hoping the hot water would still work.

Hopefully the money was transferred from my church to the landlord here.

She placed her hands underneath the shower head as the water slowly warmed up to the perfect temperature.

"Yes." She shirked, jumping with joy before yet another wince and hiss of pain escaped her. "There hasn't been hot water for two days. I am so excited." She tried to pump herself up. Staying positive and looking at positives helped… Grabbing a couple of aspirin so prepared for the shower.

Walking back, Eline twirled her pigtail with her right hand as a large smile bloomed on her face. She momentarily forgot the soreness from the previous night's punch. However, the bruise reminded her of its lingering effects when her checks shifted. Sighing, Eline hopped in the shower letting the warm water wash over the soreness and wash away the grim. She thought back to yesterday.

Eline looked up. "Listen to this, God. Even though you already know what happened, I need to tell you anyway."

She raised her hands out toward the ceiling. The water raining down on her, some droplets clinging to her finger tips before sliding down her arms towards her.

"All I wanted to do was share the gospel with that man and his girlfriend or dare I say heathen…." Looking down, Eline watched as the water went down the drain below her feet. She took a steadying breath; the stress and pain from the night before catching up with her. She leaned her forehead against the shower stall wall. Her burgundy traces hiding her eyes from view had there been anyone else there to look. "But they punched me in the face! She came out of nowhere and gave me a fright!" She shuttered and let out a small sob as tears mixed with the water falling on her. Bringing a hand up to her mouth she covered it, before bringing the same hand up to wipe at her tears. "N-Now my right cheek hurts... and I think I may- I may…" her hands and shoulders trembled as another sob escaped her lips. "-need dental work." Her brain started to rush though the scenario, why it happened, what could have been done differently. Her voice rose louder with each thought. "I wasn't interested in him. I only wanted to help. We could have talked. Why didn't I leave that couple alone?!" She took several steadying breaths, her chest heaving in the warm water. She wasn't even sure if it was tears or shower water that was currently dripping from her chin, maybe it was a mix of both. It was several minutes before she continued her prayer in a slightly calmer fashion. "I still have to learn the culture here. It's taken me some time…. It's been five months since I arrived in Aegis...." She trailed off, running a hand through her soaked hair. "I am trying to do the right thing..." She clenched her fist and lifted her head to allow the water to hit her face. She winced at the pain from her bruise, but bared with it. *When was that aspirin going to kick in?* "Most people look at me weird too. I miss my home. My parents… God why did you send me here? My white skin and freckles must seem like something out of a TV show to them."

She stood there letting the warm water soak her hair even more thoroughly.

Mom and Dad, I'm glad you are doing well. It's been a month since I heard from you. I hope the town is okay. The internet there was never the best. The closest tower is several cities away, she thought, washing her face with the warm water.

Combing her hair, she turned around, letting the warm water grace her back.

Ahh sweet relief.

Having gotten her complaints out she turned her mind back to her prayer. "God," she started, feeling her mind calm and center, "Thank you for giving me this *opportunity*… Thank you for the *aspirin*…" She sighed, closing her eyes searching for anything else in her heart she wanted to pray for. "Please guide me, how I can best reach these children of yours. Forgive the woman from last night… I don't know why she did it, but God I know you'd want me to forgive her too… Amen."

The minutes passed as she felt the hot water subside, turning lukewarm.

"Time to get out," she said.

Shutting the water off, Eline used her air blower to dry her hair. *Drying my hair is the longest part of my morning routine.*

Squeezing a gray bottle, Eline felt the cold gel in her hands as she swirled her hair back into place. She also got out a bit of her meager make-up. It had been given to her by the church to wear at special events. She carefully used the concealer to cover the bruise up. She wasn't too good at make-up, but she got it to where you'd really have to look to fully see the discoloration, otherwise it could be written off as a shadow. "Perfect!"

Eline looked around her apartment. The ocean blue colors spoke to her, calming her soul. The landlord cut her deal because of her missionary status. She opened her passport which expired at the end of the month. *I have to get that done soon*, she reminded herself.

She walked over to the small kitchen pulling out a packet of green tea and a kettle. *At least I have a stove here.*

The apartment was small with only one bedroom, a shower, kitchen, and small living room.

Ah what a busy day I have before me. She looked at her calendar on the wall.

9:30 AM Meeting with Bishop Franklin

10:30 AM Street Ministry

12:30 PM Lunch

Eline looked down at her watch, showing a time of 9:05 AM. *Where has the time gone?*

She giggled before walking over the counter grabbing her Bible.

It's about a fifteen-minute bike ride to the church. Grabbing her canister, Eline poured her green tea in before heading out.

"Are you at it again, church girl?" a young African American man asked as she walked out the door.

"I told you my name is Eline," she said, pouting lightly.

"Let me ask you this," the man said, lifting his cigarette to inhale before blowing some smoke out of one side of his mouth.

Eline observed him. He was always wearing the same thing. A red hoodie, torn denim jeans, and a pair of black sneakers.

"Why are you here?" the man asked, taking another hit off of his cigarette while scanning Eline up and down.

"Because God told us '*Go into all the world and preach the gospel to all creation*' [1] so I'm here to help. Do you want a motivational talk?" Eline asked, letting a smile escape. She paused to see if he'd answer.

The man grimaced at her and flicked the cigarette onto the ground and stomped it out before turning his eyes on to her. His tongue snaked out of the side of his mouth and licked his lips in an unsavory way.

"No? Then, I guess I'll see you, Trevor." she speedily told him as she quickened her steps to walk by him. *That guy is such a creep*, she thought to herself.

Eline walked down to the second floor of the building going outside into the city.

What a beautiful day!

The sun was shining in her face as Eline put on her glasses. Her eyes traced the brick buildings colored brown and red. The steel steps heading down and up. The duplexes made the inner city look more industrial than suburbia.

"Hey there sweetie," a woman called, sitting in a wheelchair.

Eline turned her eyes to the left to see a small woman in a wheelchair. "Hey Mrs. Hattie."

"I can smell you a mile away. You smell like honey," the old woman said, putting out her hands.

Eline smiled, grabbing Hattie's hand and holding them tightly. "Good to see you too! Here are a few dollars for some food."

Mrs. Hattie smiled, rubbing Eline's hands together. "Keep praying for this old soul."

"I will!"

She has such beautiful dark skin… Maybe it's all the sunlight. Eline walked off, getting on her bike.

Early in the morning, the cars of all shapes and sizes drove by Eline. Most of the apartments were two or three stories tall, many of them bullet ridden.

Keep it moving, she thought to herself.

Eline came up to a four-way intersection she knew fondly. It was the corner of where she got punched yesterday. *People can be so cruel in this city.*

Eline's pigtails lifted up in the wind as she flew down the hill towards the church. The colorful murals came in and out of her vision as the church came into view. *There she is!* The church was always a haven for Eline during her time in the city. She felt most at peace there as her mission was to help those in the community.

Pulling up to the church, Eline saw a few women walk out and a man. *For a Monday, it's awfully busy.*

Locking up her bike, she skipped up to the church. The large multicolored glass stretched twenty feet above ground. Opening the door, she saw the plush leather pews, purple in color with brown backing lined throughout the church.

Eline walked up as the final remnants of the prayer service were leaving the church. She waved at the families cheerfully, walking up to a large man in a white and purple robe.

"Hi, Bishop Franklin," Eline said, waving her hands up.

"Ahh Eline. How are you?"

Bishop Franklin stood six foot ten. He was a rather muscular man and a prior college basketball player. He blew out his knee in 1999 and found ministry was his new calling.

Eline looked up at the dark bald man with reverence as he was often a place of refuge in a foreign land.

"I am doing well," Eline said, smiling cheerfully. "I've been busy with college and working out in the community. I always look forward to our monthly meetings."

"Yes!" Bishop Franklin's deep voice echoed off the walls. "Let's go to my office and we can talk for some time. I have an hour blocked off today for our meeting."

Eline followed Bishop Franklin to the familiar room on the first floor. She remembered it clearly. Out of the sanctuary, to the left on the back door, go down the hallway thirty-four steps, take a right, and there was his office.

Eline took a seat, looking at the pictures of Bishop Franklin dunking on individuals and posters of his college fame. She never had the courage to ask him since she met him.

"Do you miss it?" she asked in a cheerful voice.

Franklin looked up to the wall. His younger self holding a basketball in the green and white jersey. He let out a sigh and replied. "Yes, I do. Money is essential to life but maybe God was protecting me from myself." He tented his fingers still looking intently at the image on the wall as he remembered the past. "I wanted cars and fame. God humbled me. It was the championship game right before the draft…" Franklin sighed and ran a hand over his head, "But I went up for a dunk and landed awkwardly on the way down."

Eline's eyes looked up at the picture and back at Franklin. His gaze never left the picture.

"I am sorry I asked."

"It's okay," Franklin said, smiling softly. "That had to happen. Remember everything in life is part of God's plan."

Franklin intertwined his fingers, looking at Eline with deep concern. "How are you doing in our city? You came here off of a recommendation of an old friend from my childhood. I can understand if you miss your family deeply."

Eline looked down at the floor, her smile turning to a frown. Her lip quivered as tears began to fall. "I am trying my best. I want to start a family… I want to live my life. It's hard here. The people look at me strangely like I am the plague." She took another shuddering breath trying to retain her ability to speak. Lifting her eyes heavenward she managed to keep the tears light. "What did I do to them? I am trying to help..."

Franklin looked at the teary eyed girl with compassion. "You have to understand that the people in the inner-city area are skeptical of people of your color. They see you as an oppressor more than a helping hand. You have to find a way to earn their trust. A direct approach may not be helpful."

She sniffled a bit, "I'm being me." She lifted a hand and wiped her face a bit to remove the tears that had slid down her face.

"You can be you but remember what Jesus did in the word. He was in the places where the people were. Did you go to the block party several weeks ago?"

"No, I was scared." Eline replied. "I thought I would get beat up."

"Yes, that could have happened, but you never know. God honors our courage. Young one, you have to read the word and continue to grow."

Eline felt comforted from the eyes of Franklin. She felt comfortable telling him those things she felt that burdened her. "Joshua 1:9. Be strong and courageous. Do not be afraid; do not be discouraged, for the Lord your God will be with you wherever you go." She quoted her favorite verse.

Franklin narrowed his eyes as he shifted to try and get a different angle. There was something off about Eline's face… There was a shadow on her cheek…no not a shadow…her wiping had revealed a dark spot…"What happened to your cheek?" Franklin leaned forward looking at Eline deeply.

Eline straightened up, surprised he saw it. "I was trying to talk to a man on the street and his girlfriend came out and socked me. She gave me a mean right hook to the cheek. It hurts worse than a bee's sting."

Franklin leaned back in his chair letting out a breath. He hadn't realized how naive this girl was…He felt a prick of guilt at not having properly educated her before this. "Yeah. You need to be more watchful. Your cheerful demeanor can make you seem gullible and easy to manipulate. She probably thought you were flirting with him."

"Ummm…" Eline looked up at the ceiling. "May I ask you something?"

"Go ahead and shoot," Franklin said, lifting up his chai tea.

"What does stay strapped or get clapped mean?"

Franklin caught himself before spewing up his tea. A large smile graced his face as he looked at Eline.

"What?" Eline's head tilted to the right and back to the left. She put her index finger on her lip looking puzzling at Franklin.

Franklin composed himself before laughing hard. "It means you need to have a gun. If someone comes at you… you have to be prepared. You either have to shoot first or get shot."

"So basically, that means I need to have a piece, right?" Eline smiled nervously, looking at Franklin.

"You have much to learn, Eline. Yes," he said, smiling "For you visiting our city, there are specific gun laws. You may or may not be able to get a gun. I have a friend at the police station. I will see if I can make an exception. Ultimately the decision is in their hands."

Eline nodded looking at him. I'm a bit nervous at the idea of getting a weapon…Did she really need it?

"Don't worry you probably won't get clapped. The inner city has a love for the church. A lot of young people come here looking for hope and strength. Remember, God has you but you have to be wise. No more talking to guys who are by themselves. The best way is to approach a group or stand on a box on the corner. That way you don't put yourself in an awkward situation. The women around here are protective of their men. You are white as snow…so that creates a situation."

"Yeah, tell me about it." Eline felt her cheek as it still stung with pain.

"Keep some ice on it and you will be okay. So, I have something for you. We are going to be going out today and doing a different form of ministry."

"What?" Eline looked at him with a smile.

"You remember my assistant asking for your size? Take this and put it on." Franklin handed a gym bag to Eline. "Meet me out front when you are ready."

"Okay." Eline looked down at the bag with curiosity before walking out the room.

I wonder… She walked into the women's restroom. *What is this?*

Eline opened the bag to see a medium gym outfit. The blue shirt and white colors were inviting to her. *How did he know blue was my favorite color? Maybe it was a wild guess.*

Slipping into the clothes, Eline left the room and headed to the front of the church to see Franklin in the same color outfit.

"Looking good," Franklin said. "Today we are going out as you may have guessed to play basketball around the corner."

Eline let out a deep sigh. *I am not ready for this.*

"We are going to get destroyed. Those are legit basketball players. I don't even know if I can bounce the ball."

"Don't worry I will block for you," Franklin said, laughing. "Let's go."

Franklin walked through the double doors and around the corner with Eline following behind.

The only version of basketball we played at home was freeze ball. You can dribble twice, then you have to shoot, no matter where you are. It made for ridiculous half court shots. These guys are going to do crossovers and will barrel through me. God I am going to die. Keep my ankles safe, Jesus.

'You alright? What is going on in that head of yours?" Franklin asked, slowing his pace.

Eline rounded the corner with him passing by a corner store and a giant mural with the late R&B singer Kenneth Smith greeting her. *Before this I never knew any black people. I feel like I need to get deeper into their culture. I've been a bit afraid because of my interactions but God sent me here to help. The only way I can do that is to get into their culture.* Eline took a deep breath, her legs shaking slightly. "I'm doing okay," she said to him. "nervous."

"Don't be. We are going to have a good time." Franklin put up his fist toward Eline.

Eline knew that this was a sign of friendship. She bumped her first against Franklin's.

I can do this. Her eyes looked down the street and a fence came into view.

"Let's do this," Franklin said.

"Oh, look who it is. The pastor is here to get his butt whipped again," a man in a red number 10 jersey bellowed.

"I am going to make you eat those words," Franklin replied with a grin.

Eline followed closely to Franklin. She looked at the assortment of people around her. Many of them brown and a few her skin color. *I thought I would be the only one here like me.*

"Hey, she looks like she needs to be in a religious cult or something," a woman said, laughing.

Eline turned around. "I can probably outscore you by ten." *That was a bad idea. Bad idea Eline.* A shiver ran up her spine. *I am going to die out here. This will be my graveyard. My ministry is over.*

"I like a little spunk from a snowflake," the woman winked. "See you out there."

Eline breathed a sigh of relief walking up beside Franklin. She looked up at the sign and it read. *Fourth Annual Community Basketball Challenge.* Some jerseys had church names on them and others plain.

"Alright we are ready to go, and we are the first up in five minutes. Let's stretch it out," Franklin explained.

Eline followed Franklin toward three other people with similar jerseys. A man with dreads, a young woman with dark skin and short hair, and a man with fair skin and crew cut stood in front of them.

"Nice to see you again, Pastor," the fair skinned man said, putting out his hand.

"The pleasure is all mine," Franklin replied, shaking his hand before going in for an embrace. "This is Eline, an intern for our church."

Eline walked up with a large smile. "Hi. I'm Eline."

"I'm pastor Kenneth Smith, and these are my adopted children Zachary and Melissa."

"Nice to meet all of you," Eline bowed humbly.

"Can you play?" Melissa asked. "If not, we are going to get mowed over."

"It's not about that," Zachary interrupted. "It's about building relationships with the community."

"Blah, blah, blah. I want to win. What can you do? Eh Eline?"

"I can shoot three pointers and that's about it," Eline said with a smile, trying to relax.

"So pretty much you're like Tony Mitchell of the Aegis City Dragons," Melissa crossed her arms, trying to not look upset.

"Come on now Melissa, let's be nice" Kenneth looked over at his daughter with a disapproving glance.

"Alright, Dad. I got it. Don't blame me if we lose because of her."

This one is a tough one to crack. Eline looked around the squared area to see four different colors of jerseys. Her eyes traced green, yellow, and red.

The red team looks the most intimating. Green looks speedy, and yellow looks all like me a bit weak.

Eline was gazing at the teams when she felt a tap on her shoulder.

"Here take an *Oh Snap*," Zachary said.

Eline looked down at the orange color drink cold to the touch.

Zachary's smile was warm as he held up the bottled beverage toward Eline. Eline grabbed the drink and tapped it with the green bottle Zachary was holding.

"Let's do this," Zachary said in a calm voice.

"Alright everyone let's get this party started," a small man said standing on a box with a megaphone. "The tournament will be full court and single elimination. The first team to get to 50 points will win. If you lose your out, no retry. The final two teams will pick their best free throw shooter. The winner will get a year pass for two free meals to Betty's Ridiculous Burgers for their whole team. We will have a forty-five-minute time limit. First up we have the green versus the blue team."

"Those burgers are the business," Melissa said, stepping onto the court.

Eline felt like her heart almost shook out her chest as the subwoofers blared a mix of dubstep and hip hop. She stepped up towards the middle of the course looking at a tall man with tattoos, a squared shaped chin and a green number 18 jersey.

"You at the wrong place little one. We going to give you the ball first. Look at those sneakers. Budget. My kicks are name brand baby."

Eline passed the ball, checking it with the large man. Her eyes looked to the left and right as the whistle blew. Her eyes quickly glance to the left toward Melissa, wide open to the left. *Okay remember the bounce pass to my brother.* Eline gripped the ball pushing it towards Melissa.

"Nice pass!" Melissa shouted, speeding down the court. Eline followed, trying to keep up with the large man chasing towards Melissa.

"I got you, Melissa," Franklin spread his arms, blocking the large man with a pick.

Melissa crossed the ball to the left and looked back at Eline as she was running to the middle of the court and towards the top of the three-point marker. Melissa's eyes looked back at the net several feet away from her. She ran towards the basket, putting the ball in her right hand before pushing the ball behind her back and bouncing it towards Eline.

Eline's eyes widened.

A no look pass…no way.

Eline opened her hands as she felt the ball bounce into her hand with intense speed. A stacked woman in a green number 34 jersey ran toward her. *I can't shoot.* Eline turned her shoulder to the woman striking a defensive stand. Looking back toward the front of the three-point line, Zachary looked at her. To the right was Franklin being covered by a tall guy in a green number 19 jersey.

Eline looked at Zachary, who was outrunning a girl in the green number 35 jersey, before passing the ball to him.

Zachary grabbed the ball, smiling. Posting up before he shot the ball at the basket.

SWOOSH!

"What an excellent three-point show and play by… what shall we call her?" the DJ asked. "I'll call her Mrs. Pigtails."

Eline heard the cheers as she felt a slight push.

"Lucky first try, chump!" the woman said before stomping off.

The time passed as the game proceeded back and forth.

Eline looked up at the clock past the thirty-minute mark. *She looked at the court standing out the lines. It's 34 to 31. We are behind by three. I'm exhausted.* Eline wiped the sweat off her head. Pushing the ball out, she felt herself stumble a bit.

"Wrong move girl," the large woman stepped in front of Zachary before grabbing the ball and slamming it into the hoop.

"I don't—" Eline whispered as she felt herself start to fall.

30 minutes later, Eline opened her eyes slowly.

"You alright there newbie?" Melissa asked, looking down at her.

"Wh— What happened?" Eline looked around at the court.

"We had to forfeit because you were unable to play," Franklin explained. "It's okay. We had a strong showing. We will get them next year."

"Now that you are feeling better can you get off me," Melissa added.

It took Eline a moment to realize that Melissa had lent her her lap to cusion her head while she was out. "Oh sorry!" Eline stood up, blushing slightly. "Thank you for doing that for me."

"I'm not heartless you know." Melissa stood up, stretching. "I want to dunk on the red team so bad. There is a guy who used to make fun of me years ago in grade school." Melissa clinched her fist looking back at the basketball court.

"Don't worry, my daughter, you will get them next time," Kenneth said smiling.

"That happy Christian stuff. I get it. We have to be good sports. That doesn't mean I can't dunk on these fools and break ankles. I'm in my early twenties!"

"I am still your father, child," Kenneth said, smiling gently.

"Drink this, Eline." Franklin handed her an *Oh Snap* that looked like a grape flavor.

"Thank you!" Eline opened the bottle, sipping it quickly. *Refreshing! I love grape flavored things.*

'We ought to get going, everyone," Kenneth said. "Honestly, I didn't expect us to do as well as we did. That bass is starting to get to me. These old ears can only take so much music. "

"Likewise," Franklin said, putting his arms around him for an embrace. "See you guys."

Zachary and Melissa waved while walking away with their father from the basketball court.

Eline looked around before sitting up, her eyes met the woman from before the game.

She is going to come and chew me out. She is going to say I am rubbish at this sport, Eline thought, preparing for the worst.

"Hey snowflake!" she said with a loud voice. "You alright with me. You came out here and spent time with us. You got your butt whipped. It's the thought that counts."

Eline smiled before standing. "It's a pleasure," she said, putting out her fist.

The woman shook her head. "One step at a time, I suppose. Turn your fist the other way, snowflake."

Eline laughed and turned her fist to meet the muscular woman.

"The name is Serena. This block and ten blocks up and down are my area. You won't have any problems talking about your gospel to my people. Keep your wits about you."

Eline nodded as the woman walked off.

"Hey snowflake," Serena said, looking back. "Your name now is E."

"You got it," Eline said, putting up her thumb.

Franklin looked at Eline with a smile. "See? You're getting it now. You have to immerse yourself in their world. I can't do it for you. You went out there and took some hits and elbows. They saw your tenacity. Respect is earned here in the streets."

Eline looked at the stern look from Franklin. *He can be scary when he wants to be.*

"Thank you for that. That dunk you put on that small guy was awesome."

"You liked that huh?" Franklin said. "I laid it on thick. They can stop me when I go in. I have to be careful though. I usually only dunk once per game."

"I can see why." Eline opened her phone. "I need to get home and shower. I will have lunch with a friend soon."

"Let's head back to the church," Franklin said smiling.

God, I did it. I finally found a connection. Basketball is like freeze ball but more intense. It's like being in a real professional game. Some of those individuals should play in the minor league. They ran circles around me. They were probably being nice. I did get a few moves on them, Eline thought to herself, satisfied with today's outcome.

Eline rounded the last corner with Franklin who was quiet for most of the walk.

"You okay, Franklin?" Eline looked up at him.

"Yeah. I'm okay, tired. After yesterday's service I was in a counseling session with a couple for hours. It was draining. Last night I couldn't sleep. It's nothing. That's life."

"You sure?" Eline asked, looking up to him.

"I'm good, but thank you for your concern. Get to your friend. I have more free time so we will try to have weekly meetings instead of monthly meetings."

"That sounds good," Eline replied, unlocking her bike lock. "I'll see you."

Eline waved, stepping on her bike.

Okay! I am still pretty winded. I am going to have to push it up the hill.

Eline looked up the hill pushing her bike at a fast pace. *Don't push too hard!* Eline breathed heavily and reached the top of the hill. Looking back down she heaved a sigh of relief. *I should have taken a train. I feel like I am going to pass out.*

Eline walked over to the lock bay putting her double lock on her bike wheel. *Ugh I need to take a quick shower.* Eline ran up the stairs and opened her door. Slipping out her clothes she ran into the shower and turned the water on. *I need some cold water after all of that.*

She glanced at the small digital clock and saw that the time is 12:05.

Eline jumped in the shower the cold water hitting her. *I have five minutes to get clean and five minutes to get dressed. I can do it!* Eline grabbed her soap and scrubbed her body clean. *I need to get better at basketball.*

The minutes flew by as Eline turned the water off. Jumping out she dried her hair, touched up her make up and slipped on her clothes. Eline heard her phone rumble.

That's probably Samantha.

Eline grabbed her phone as it showed 12:20 pm. Walking out her door, she packed her mace and went down the stairs.

Eline walked out to see cars speeding down the road at a high speed.

That's odd. Why were they going so fast?

Eline unhooked her bike and started up towards 29th street.

"Oh my god!" Eline swerved to the left as a car ran up on the curb, almost hitting her and continued down the road. "What is going on?"

Eline looked off into the distance as she saw a person in the car shaking violently.

Distracted, another car swerved near Eline, narrowly missing her before crashing into a wall. She could see that the person inside was injured but not dead. She quickly ran toward it to help.

"Are you okay?" Eline shouted, looking through the windows.

The man in the passenger seat waved, unhooking his seatbelt.

Eline's eyes widened in horror as she watched the man have his neck ripped out by a person behind his seat. *Oh my God… what?*

Eline stumbled, her legs falling underneath her. *Why would she bite his neck out?* Eline felt as if she would faint.

The deranged woman then slammed her head into the front glass furiously.

Eline stood, her legs shaking as she watched the woman slam her head over and over into the windshield. The deranged woman managed to break through the car glass, shards of glass was sticking through her head, unhindered by the pain. She screamed at Eline, her blood curdling moans sent shivers down Eline's spine.

Eline, shaking off the fear from the horrific image, managed to run into a nearby apartment.

Chapter 4

June 1st, 2015

Aegis City – 29th Street Downtown

1230

Stay calm Daren. Okay? This could be a bad dream, or this could be the end times.

Daren looked out the window watching the cars zoom by and the alarm blaring. Looking over at the tv, he watched the screen shift to a blue screen with white letters.

THE MAYOR IS DEAD. STAY INDOORS. POTENTIAL BIO-TERRORIST ATTACK IN PROGRESS.

"The mayor is dead," Daren whispered, looking around his room for his bat.

There is something going on. I need to find Michael. He is the only family I truly care about. He's like a brother to me. He wouldn't abandon me. Where is he?

Daren went to the kitchen grabbing a large kitchen knife and wasp spray. He ran around the pantry, grabbing fruit and some beverages to slam into his bag.

I'm coming to you cousin.

Daren ran out the door watching people huddled in the doorway.

"Something is happening out there. You shouldn't go," the man said, trying to hold Daren back.

"Let me go, man. My cousin is out there. I'll be fine."

Daren pushed past the hysterical man running down the stairs. Daren heard tires skid as he turned the corner heading down the black stairs. Opening the door, he heard a woman scream.

"They're crazy!" the woman yelled, running by Daren with blood on her ankles.

God. What the heck am I walking into?

'Help me!" Daren heard a female voice yell from the front of the apartment door that was wide open. Daren ran up to see a woman with dark pigtails running toward him.

God give me strength. Not far behind the pigtailed girl was another woman. Though this one was screaming in an erially, unnatural way, arms outstretched with blood dripping off of her head, and mouth. Something shiny was sticking out of her head… Her movements seemed off too… This crazed woman was starting to run right for him.

"Get behind me!" Daren yelled to the frightened brunette. Eline didn't need to be told twice as she ducked behind him. Daren ran up to meet the bloodied woman holding the bat. "Get back! I'm warning you."

The crazed woman ran at Daren undetured.

"I warned you," Daren spoke with authority. Clenching his bat Daren stepped to the side and slammed it into the side of the woman's head knocking her to the ground. More blood pooling around her from the injuries.

"What the heck?" Daren looked back at the Eline behind him in shock. "You okay?" he breathed out numbly.

"Yeah." Eline muttered hands on her knees panting.

"What is your name?" Daren asked.

"It's Eline," she said, looking at him, "Th- Th-Thank you." "I'm Daren." He introduced when a movement behind him shifted his attention. Turning to look down, Daren watched as the crazed woman started to twitch and try to get up. "Don't get up, I'm warning you."

The woman pushed up from the ground stumbling slightly. Her head hung downward, limply. Her body was moving in jerky motions like being pulled harshly by invisible strings.

Daren pushed forward, raising his bat into the air and slammed it forcefully into the woman's head twice. He felt the muscles in his arm burn as he slammed the edge of the bat four more times in the woman's head. There was a sickening splat and crack as the woman's skull split open. More blood rushing out.

"Oh my God!" Eline yelled, her face pale, looking at Daren. "You killed her!"

Daren looked back, his eyes widened. "I had to. She was going to kill you."

Eline fell to the ground putting her arms over herself muttering "Oh my God, oh my God… " Eline closed her eyes slumping over.

Daren looked back at Eline's unconscious form on the ground. He was still numb from what had occured, strange things were happening he needed to keep moving… *I can't leave her here.* Daren walked over to Eline, picking her up he walked back into his building. *I can't leave her. Michael. I will be coming soon. I have to help this woman. Not even noticing the other people still huddled in the foyer, Daren arrived at the elevator.* He shifted the girl in his arms along with the bat he still held to press the second button as he walked out the door and headed down the hall.

Setting Eline down, he opened his door, picked her back up and walked in. He laid her gently on the couch and locked his door. He'd stay with her. *Okay, I need to think quickly. If those things make it up here, I need to be ready to go.*

Daren put his book bag down and pulled his shelf toward the front door. With that done Daren finally allowed himself a moment to think. *I have enough food for a few days, but I will need to be on the move soon.* Glancing at Eline Daren ran a hand through his hair nervously, *Hopefully, she can make it as well. I can't stay too long. Jesus. Is this the end of the world?*

Daren went back to the TV. *Maybe there is some updated news.* Daren turned the volume down. He took a blanket and covered Eline and felt her head. *She is not hot or anything. She is still breathing. Probably in shock.*

Daren lifted up her head slowly and put a blue pillow underneath it. *She's quite pretty, actually.*

Flipping through the channels the same blue screen was pictured. It simply read, "Nowhere is safe." *Nowhere is safe. That can't be true. The whole city is screwed. I refuse to believe it. Where is the military? Where is the police force? How is all of this spreading? Who would do this to our city?*

Daren flipped through the channels rapidly on the remote. It must of been at least a hundred times he hit the button but saw nothing but that blue screen or static... *This is hopeless. We have no answers.* Daren lifted his head as the TV showed two words.

SHATTERED EXPECTATIONS

The words in white said in the darkness. It blinked three times before the screen went blue.

Shattered Expectations. What does that mean? Maybe it's useless words or a glitch in the system. Daren felt a stir behind him as he heard a soft female voice.

"Thank you," Eline said softly.

"You okay?" Daren asked, walking to the kitchen.

"I guess this is your apartment," Eline said, sitting up slowly, rubbing her head.

"You shouldn't sit up so quickly," Daren said, heating up some water in the kitchen.

"You saved me," Eline said, looking around the apartment. "Are you a minister?"

"I was training to become a chaplain, but it seems the world has different plans."

"This is the work of the Devil," Eline said, trying to concentrate. She put her hand on her head, rubbing her temples.

"Here." Daren walked over with a blue mug. "It's green tea. I keep some when I get sick. With everything you've been through I thought it would help you relax."

"Thanks," Eline said, grabbing the cup gently. "Any news on the TV?"

"Nothing useful, except the same message over and over. The mayor is dead," Daren said, looking at her.

"Wow!" Eline shook her head, slowly her eyes flowed with tears. "Is this across the world or here? What is going on?"

"Calm down, we have to keep a level head," Daren said sharply. "I am as concerned as you."

"Franklin!" Eline shouted in panic, trying to stand. "I wonder what happened to him?"

"You mean Bishop Franklin at the church down the street?" Daren looked at her with curiosity.

"He's like a mentor of mine. I need to see if he's okay." Eline took a sip of her tea curling up in the blanket. "Thank you! Really! But, I need to get to the church."

"I wouldn't do that. You've been out for a while." Daren pulled out his phone, showing Eline a video of the outside.

"They are like crazed humans and out of their minds. What is going on with them? It's like they lost their traits of humanity." Eline watched the video three times over, eyes growing rounder each time.

"They seem to be attracted by noise," Daren said. "I was watching outside when a person was running by and the crazed person chased them down. They seem to have the ability to run without tiring."

"I saw one transform," Eline said.

Daren looked at her with sincere concern. "Transform?"

"Yeah." Eline put down her tea and idally started to twirl one of her pigtails. "It was horrifying. One moment the woman was jerking around. The next moment she was biting a man's neck and then she rammed her head so hard into the glass that she busted it out...." she paused looking down, "You know the rest."

"Yeah." Daren looked over at his bat still covered in blood.

Lifting her gaze she followed Daren's line of sight to the bat. "Is that steel?" Eline asked, looking at him.

"Yeah. It won't break. I only have one other weapon, a long knife that I was going to take with me. I was going to find my cousin, Michael."

"I want to go find my friend, Franklin." Eline breathed heavily, looking down at the tea. "Can you help me?"

She's nice but I need to find Michael. Daren sighed, looking at her. "We both have people we want to get to. The streets are a no go. They are swarming with those things. They are standing around. When a car drives by it alerts them because of the noise and they all flock to it. I heard a few gunshots and then screaming. It's like some horror movie out there." Daren took a sip of his water looking at her.

"We could take the rooftops," Eline spoke in a soft tone. "I'm from the country and I am really good at climbing and scouting. There was nothing but miles of land where I am from."

"Where exactly is that?" Daren asked, looking at her with curiosity.

"It's across the ocean, in a small town"

Daren and Eline sat up straight when they heard a loud bang at the door.

"Stay quiet," Daren said, going to the kitchen and shutting off the light.

BANG, BANG

The gunshots rang.

"No! No! How could you?" a woman screamed from the hallway.

"You're next!" a man said before a single gunshot rang out.

Daren got closer to the door as he heard someone wiggle the handle slightly.

"It's locked," the man said.

The footsteps faded as Daren walked back slowly toward the sofa.

"People are already killing each other out there," Eline said in a somber tone. "The anger you showed when killing that woman is chilling. You don't even know me. How could you do that?"

"I had no choice. You needed help." Daren's hands shook slowly, putting down the bat and sitting on the sofa. "That's the first time I truly felt my life was in danger. Living on this side of town there are a lot of gang bangers. I never felt too unsafe. Today, I started feeling comfortable."

"Let me tell you where I am from," Eline said.

"I didn't recognize that accent. You said you were from across the sea?" Daren mused, putting his hand on his chin. He was eager to hear more, maybe release some tension by getting to know one another.

Eline nodded, still shaking from the loud bang. "I am from Millington on the Royal Victorian Harbor. It's a small fishing town. The closest major city is two hundred miles away. That is where the closest airport is. It's a small mining town. I'm here to help my family. I fear they are dead. What if this situation is worldwide? What if this is God's judgement on us for the sin of man?"

"You have got to stay positive," Daren said with a smile. "I know it's hard."

Eline tried to smile. "I think we should lay low until the evening. You need to rest. We can talk and develop a game plan. The news said we should hunker down, but I am not going to stay put and die. If twenty men or gang members rush that door. I can't take all of them."

"We have to stay mobile then," Eline said solemnly. "Okay, I am going to stay positive."

Eline let go a shaky smile. "I can change. I'm a bit of a scaredy cat but I am true as they come. Let's get this win, Daren."

Daren smiled, sipping his water. "Get some rest. I will take my first watch and try to pick something up on an old radio."

"What about you? I'm good. I got a full night's rest yesterday plus I am still amped up." Daren smiled gently, walking to the window.

God, what am I going to do? Daren leaned on the window as the minutes passed. He heard the slight snore of Eline grow louder. *She must be tired. I'm still in shock. Get it together, Daren. God lead his people in battles in the Bible. But am I a murderer? That thing was only a shell. The soul was gone.*

Daren looked out to see the street line with people. Some of them dead, others standing silently in circles.

I wonder... Daren went to the kitchen to grab a cup. Opening his window quietly before he slung the mug into the middle of the four-lane road. *As I thought.*

Daren watched the crazed individuals run towards the broken mug and stand there in a huddle.

So, they are attracted by sound for sure. Without sound they remain still as a church mouse. I wonder how their sense of smell is? They seem to be crazy humans and they twitch violently when noise is around them. I guess I'll call them twitchers.

Daren watched as the twitchers walked slowly away from the mug in different directions. Closing the window, he saw a young girl and her mother walk outside the apartment across the street. *No, don't do it.* Daren watched in horror as the young girl hit a loose brick near the stairs of the building. *No… No…*

Daren watched in dread as ten twitchers descended upon the duo. He closed the window as their screams echoed throughout the cluttered intersection.

There was nothing I could do. God, I can't save everyone. I have one person in my care I can protect. That is what I am going to do.

Daren turned around, looking at Eline with tears in his eyes. *Michael would want me to get her to safety too. My cousin can take care of himself. He is a strong man. Okay, God. I am going to get her to safety and come back to find Michael. But what is safe now?*

Daren sat back on the couch as he sat down. His eyes slowly closed, and he drifted off to sleep.

Several hours later, Daren opened his eyes slowly as he looked over at the couch beside him.

Where is Eline?

"You said you were keeping first watch, silly," Eline said from the kitchen.

Daren put his hand on his chest. "I thought something had happened to you or you left. I was afraid you jumped out of the window and tried to find Franklin."

"I am no good on my own. Plus, I like being around you. You're interesting. Despite being a Christian, you seem quite focused though not as cheerful as me. You seem to keep people at a distance."

"People here can be difficult to live with. You have to have tough skin to live in the inner-city," Daren said standing up.

What is she cooking? Daren peered over the counter at the stove.

"I hope you like fish," Eline said. "I found some in your freezer and I thought it would be best to have a meal before we come up with a plan."

Daren didn't feel like smiling. He killed a woman today. He felt the pressure of bashing her skull in. *God, what I have done.*

Eline looked over at him. "What's on your mind?"

"Am I evil? I bashed that woman's head in repeatedly and now I am going to sit down and eat a meal. I need to atone for my sins."

"You need to atone for nothing," Eline said, putting the plates on the small table in the living room.

Eline walked over, grabbing Daren's hand and guiding him to the table. "Here. Sit silly. That's my nickname for you. It's silly. You can't argue it. Once I've made up my mind, that's final."

Daren looked down at the baked fish, mash potatoes, macaroni and cheese, and glass of water.

What did I do to deserve this? Where did this woman come from? I hope she remembers to spice up the food.

Daren took a deep breath. Looking at Eline he smiled. "Thank you for Eline, father God. Thank you for her kindness. Keep our minds sharp and hearts steady. Give us wisdom on who to trust and what to do in this time. Amen."

"You're welcome! Amen." Eline took a bite of fish, her cheeks lighting up. "It's how my mom made it."

"What do you know about cooking fish?" Daren said, taking a bite.

This is delicious.

Eline looked up back from her plate, her eyes tracing Daren's every bite.

"What did you use to spice the fish?" Daren asked, taking another bite. "It's so tender. I have never had fish this soft."

"We use something called sand spice where I am from. I keep some on me wherever I go. It was the most expensive thing to carry with me from overseas and I am glad I was able to pay for it," Eline said, clapping her hands together softly.

"What is sand spice?" Daren asked.

"There is a beach that has edible salt. It's like sea salt but it doesn't taste as nasty. What we do is bring it to our houses and boil the salt. We bring the salt and boil it in water. We then let it sit and drain it in a pouch. It's like a rub. We don't overuse it. We understand that the earth is God's kingdom. We use it only for celebrations and birthdays."

"That's a unique way to live," Daren said. "In our city, it's all about consumption. Who can make the biggest and greatest thing? Money, Money, Money."

"We have money problems too across the sea," Eline said, finishing up her fish. "That could all be gone. Nothing could be left of my village. "

"We don't know for sure. Communications seem to be stagnated, but the power is still on." Daren looked down at his phone. It was 10:30 PM. "I was out for so long."

"You needed the rest. After taking out that crazy woman you need your heart to be full and to think clearly." Eline smiled, taking a sip of the water.

Daren nodded, looking over at his phone as it flashed a yellow box. "I got a message. It's from Michael!"

Cousin, I love you. Everything is pretty bad down here. People are killing each other. I am okay. Can't talk long. Try to get to the countryside of the city where the new homes are being built. It's like they are losing their minds and people are robbing each other. I'm armed and already had to kill two people. One was crazy looking and the other was a looter. Get to the countryside to Aunt May's house. We may not be close to her but that's the safest place I can think of. Bye.

Daren held the phone, putting it to his head. "Michael is alive. Thank God." *Why didn't I think of texting him?*

"Our destination is your aunt's house?" Eline questioned.

Daren nodded, "Yes, there was a falling out with the family a while ago. She is a kind woman, stubborn, but she wouldn't turn away family. At least I hope not."

"What about the police?" Eline asked, leaning forward, and moving her hands out to punctuate the group. "What about the military?" She emphasized with her hands and voice raising a notch "Where are they?"

"Who knows?" Daren signed looking down at what was left of his fish. *She has the same thoughts I did earlier today*... "They could have been attacked as well. Nothing makes sense but I am not going to stick around and die in the city."

"I'm glad your cousin is alive. Hopefully, Franklin made it out," Eline said, a soft sob escaping her lips at the thought of what could be happening to him.

"Franklin is a strong man, and I wouldn't want to mess with him," Daren said, feeling optimistic.

Eline wiped her tears, looking at him, trying to feel confident. "Anyway, I had an idea about defense. If we need to protect ourselves, we need to use the round trash can lids as shields. We can push them back if one tries to corner us—"

"I call them twitchers," Daren said.

"Good name," Eline said. "Is it because they twitch around when they walk and chase people?"

"Exactly. And you saw first-hand how the woman's neck frantically twitched after killing her husband," Daren said. "That's a good idea about the trash can lids. Let me check something."

Daren walked to his bedroom walking back with a box. "I think what we need is here."

Eline looked at him with curiosity. Her head went back and forth watching Daren search through the box. "What are you looking for, silly?"

"Ah yes." Daren pulled out a large bag. "These are zip ties. I used these when I volunteered in college at a corrections facility."

"Like restraints in a way." Eline nodded fiercely.

"Like that. We can use these as a handle for the trash can lids. We can zip them together and hold it in the middle. This way we can put them on our backs and hold them in our right hands like a shield."

"Great idea. We can use that to push through." Eline said standing. "That's a great defense. Do you have another bat or anything I can use? All I have is mace in my bag."

"You can have this knife." Daren said, walking over to his bag. "It's a hunting knife and it's quite sharp. It was a gift from my father when he was in the military. He used it to kill a man once."

Eline took the knife from Daren. She ran her fingers across the initials "D.S.Sr. You're a Jr. then?" Eline asked.

"Yeah," Daren said, smiling. "My parents were wonderful people."

"Were?" Eline asked.

"Yeah," Daren said looking at his phone. "Let's get everything packed up. It's time to go."

Chapter 5

June 2nd, 2015

Aegis City – 29th Street Downtown

12:15 A.M.

Daren nodded at Eiline, looking at her with concern. "Are you ready to go?" Eline was standing with a trash can lid on her right hand and gloves on her hands. "When we leave here there is no turning back."

"I'm ready," Eline said with intensity.

Daren pushed the dresser slowly towards them and opened the door. His eyes looked up and down the hallway. *Two stairs toward the top and the elevator. The elevator makes too much noise.* "Make sure your phone is on silent, Eline." He whispered, realizing they forgot to check on that before leaving.

Daren stepped out into the hallway turning left gripping his bat intensely with both hands.

The hallway was silent.

Daren saw the woman and man who were murdered several hours earlier. Their blood covered most of the hallway as Daren and Eline walked slowly past them stepping quietly. *God, keep my hands steady. I am so scared.*

Daren looked back at Eline. Her eyes were wide open, similar to having drank twelve cups of coffee. The scent of death permeated the air and filled their lungs. Hearts pounding, each step they took seemed louder in their own ears than in real life. The twitchers could be anywhere, and frightened people that were killing indiscriminately were about too. One sound and they were dead. One sound would be all it took… One sound.

Walking forward slowly the hallway felt like a mile long. Daren and Eline creeped down the hallway slowly passing by the numbers on the wall. Their eyes met every number with anticipation. 221, 222, 223, 224. They creeped toward the T shape intersection. Daren turned around, looking at Eline. Daren leaned into her ear. "We are going to go left and up the backstairs to the roof. Let me check the corner."

Eline nodded looking at him with care as she put up her trashcan shield. She swallowed, eyes alert, heart pounding. The silence was deafening.

Daren walked forward one step, his eyes peering around the corner. *Oh. God no. Not now.*

He turned back to Eline, whispering in her ear. "There is a twitcher around the corner, chowing down." His own voice even though soft seemed much louder in the stillness.

Eline leaned in close to Daren's ear. "Maybe it will continue eating on its snack and we can sneak by."

Daren shook his head. "Too much of a risk to take. I don't want to make any noise even though there is only one of them."

Daren took another peek around the corner to see another twitcher walk out of the room.

A shout from behind them made them both jump. "Oh shoot!"

Daren turned back looking at Eline's sweet smile as he saw four men at the end of the stairs by his apartment. They were armed with melee weapons and were doing nothing to remain quiet. "Oh gosh." He hissed. His heart hammered at the sounds and implications.

"Look what we have here." The man's voice thundered across the space. He licked his lips, noticing the girl. "Get the bitch and kill the guy," the large man commanded, holding a hunting knife.

The sounds would bring the twitcher and these men were definitely not going to be allies. Throwing caution to the wind, Daren shouted, "Run Eline!" He darted to the right as he ran as hard as he could with Eline close in tow.

"I got you," Eline said, running past Daren to be in front of him, slamming her plastic can lid into the face of the twitcher and running by it without missing a beat.

Daren didn't have time to be impressed as he gripped his bat and swung into the second twitcher face. The blood covered the metal bat. "Keep moving!" he yelled to Eline.

Eline ran towards the stairwell, only two apartments left to pass, as three men rounded the corner thirty feet behind them.

Daren saw the stair door come into view as he heard a growling at the final apartment door. *The twitcher! Let this work!* "Eline, go!" He shouted once more.

Eline ran past the final apartments, slamming the stairwell door open with a *BANG!* She then started heading up the stairs rapidly.

Daren sprinted across the hallway opening the final door as he saw five twitchers dart out of the room. Daren turned and went through the doorway and stood still for a moment. Thump, thump, thump, his heart was demanding he move. But he wanted to be sure his plan worked...

"Oh shit!" He heard one of the men yell as he looked through the small glass window of the stairwell door. His plan had worked. The four creeps were fighting for their lives as the twitchers descended on them.

Daren turned around and started to run upstairs after Eline. *Two more floors to go.* Daren grabbed the stairwell handlebars darting up the stairs as she saw Eline waiting at the top for him.

Eline jumped forward wrapping her arms around him. "Don't do that silly!" she whispered releaf evident in her voice in his ear. "You could have gotten yourself killed."

Daren felt a large smile grace his face as he returned the hug. "Thank you for caring for me." He said softly. "We are on the fourth floor."

Eline grabbed at his shoulder. "We have to be careful. Someone could be setting a trap or there could be twitchers up here."

Daren knew the risks and he nodded. *Either way it's a death trap. We could run into a bunch of twitchers or a gang.* "We have to go," Daren said, looking at her with a somber expression. Daren pushed open the door as he stepped out slowly. A click and a deep voice were his greeting.

"Take one more step and I will blow your head off," a male voice threatened.

Daren felt the cold steel pressed against the side of his head. *Is this the end? Do I swing the bat or run for it? I can't outrun a bullet.*

"Turn slowly to the right so I can look into your eyes to make sure you aren't one of them or turning into one. Do it now," the man said in a cool aggressive tone.

Daren turned to the right looking at the man with the flashlight in one hand and a gun in another.

"Daren," the man sounded relieved. "It's me Ken from the first floor."

Daren breathed his own sigh of relief. "We good man?" he asked, looking at Ken.

"Yeah brother, we good," Ken said walking back a few paces, the gun now resting barrel to the floor at his side.

"It's alright Eline." Daren walked forward as Eline followed him.

Ken's eyes widened a bit, "Who's the pretty little thing you got with you, Daren? I didn't know you liked them white like snow," Ken said, letting go a rough chuckle.

"I like all flavors," Daren bantered. "God created all of us in his image."

"I know I know," Ken stated, lifting the hand holding the flashlight to wave it off. He rolled his eyes a bit.

"You almost got a slap to your face," Eline said, eyeing Ken a bit huffy with her arms crossed.

"Your boy almost got a bullet to the temple." He countered. "You'll be grateful," I asked. I could have blown him away. I can't kill a man without asking first what he did." Ken crossed his own arms looking up at the moon.

"Is it you up here?" Daren put his hand on his chest trying to calm his heart rate.

"Yeah, it's me. A dead couple is over there. One of them has a cross bow and then I found a gun on the other. Do you know anyone who can use a crossbow?"

Eline looked at Ken with a small smile. "I can. We used them all the time to hunt back home."

"Say that again," Ken said. "That accent is fire baby. You're lighting up my soul."

"Flattery will get you nowhere," Eline said. "Are you sure they're dead?" Eline looked back at Ken.

"I'm sure," Ken nodded, trying to sound helpful.

Eline disappeared around the corner of the rooftop looking for the dead couple and a new weapon to help them in their journey.

"Those pick-up lines are not working, man. I don't think those would work at any time."

"I can't help but try." Ken said.

Daren eyed Ken. *It's been years since I've seen him. He bulked up a bit. His biceps are twice as much as mine. I guess he kept hitting the gym and went into boxing like he wanted.*

"I found it," Eline said, skipping back over to the entrance to the rooftop.

Crack! Crack! Crack!

"That's gunfire," Ken said hurriedly. "Get down."

"Where did it come from?" Eline looked around trying to ascertain the direction of the bullets.

"I think it came from down the road." Daren walked slowly to the edge of the roof top to see a large pick-up truck with five men on it.

Eline and Ken followed and watched another truck pull up.

"Let them have it!" They heard a man yell from the back of the first truck raising a stick-like object above his head. A gun? Then, music started to blare out the speakers as dozens of twitchers ran toward the noise.

The lyrics blared with a heavy bass through the speakers. "Clap them cheeks, make 'em moist, lay it on thick, and do that thing."

Crack! Crack! Crack! Gun fire started to sound from below.

"That music is repulsive," Eline whispers looking over at Daren. "Who would sing such music? Music is supposed to have a meaning?"

"I guess the meaning is to get women in a bad way," Daren said with a disapproving look. He didn't like the lyrics either.

Crack! Crack! Crack! Gun fire continued to sound from below.

"That beat is hard though," Ken said, bopping his shoulders.

"I can't lie. The beat is hard," Daren said, trying not to smile.

The bullets rang though as the twitchers that were populating all laid dead in the street. "Good shooting!" a man on the truck yelled out.

Boom! A single bullet shot rang out as one of the men in the back of the truck fell dead.

"Oh!" Ken gasped, dropping to lie down. "That was a sniper shot. Get down y'all!"

The trio laid silent on their backs. They heard two more sniper shots and heard the truck speed off.

"What the hell was that?" Ken asked, crawling over to the cover near the rooftop door.

Eline and Daren followed, staying low to the ground.

"I don't think they are trying to kill us. If they wanted to, they probably could have popped us off easily," Ken said. "That made my heart jump."

"I thought the only thing that made your heart jump was me," Eline said in a joking manner, but the smile didn't reach her eyes.

"You got jokes kid, alright. You're alright with me, Eline. I got your back. You can roll with me."

Daren shook his head looking at the ground. *What a mess.*

"Where are y'all headed to?" Ken asked, looking at the moon.

"We are going to his aunt's house," Eline said in a cheerful manner.

"You're awfully happy," Daren said, trying to calm himself down. *You would think these gunshots would bother me. Death is staring me in the face. God, give me strength. Am I really doing this? Where's Michael? I could use his calm voice right now.*

"Where is your aunt's house, Daren?"

"She has one of the new homes outside of town. We figured we could get there and think about what to do next."

Ken frowned, eyeing the air sternly. "You're going to do all of that without guns. You got a trash can lid, a crossbow with twenty arrows, and a steel bat." He assessed looking at them like they had lost it.

Ken looked at Eline and Daren up and down. He sighed and shrugged his shoulders "I guess I need to come with you guys. I've got two magazines and a first aid kit in my backpack that I found off a police officer on the first floor."

"Welcome to the group," Eline said, putting out her fist towards Ken.

"Alright Eline I see you. I am going to call you Little E." Ken put out his fist, lightly tapping hers.

"What's the plan, Daren? You seem to have a firm idea where to go," Ken said, looking at him re-crossing his arms.

"Eline and I were going to cross the rooftops and get as far as we can until we can't. I imagine we can get to 42nd street. Who knows? We are going to get as far as we can."

"Let's get going then," Ken said, winking at Eline.

He is such a flirt. Daren mentally rolled his eyes.

Eline grabbed Daren's hand as they proceeded to the edge of the rooftop.

"It looks like a two-foot jump," Daren said, looking down at the ground four stories up. He looked up at the moon as it's shine glinted across the rooftops as if painting a path for them.

Daren looked at Eline whose cheeks had a unique calmness to them. *How can she be so calm? I know that she is scared to death.*

Daren felt the warmth of her hand as he let go gently. "I will be the first to go." Daren stepped back a little bit and ran forward, clearing the gap with ease.

"You think you might be showing off a little bit there," Ken said with a light chuckle.

"Oh, shut it. He is trying to lead." Eline said looking over to him with a pouty expression. She looked at the gap and pressed her feet down into the payment and jumped. Her feet touched down on the other side as she had cleared the gap.

"You didn't even get a running start," Daren said, looking at her with awe and curiosity.

"Didn't need one." Eline said smiling. "I used to clear gaps larger than that while hiking through the countryside of our town. People half my age used to jump those types of gaps with their eyes closed."

Daren shook his head. "Way to hit me with the gut right there." He lightly stroked his hand on his gut.

"You can take it silly," Eline said with a small chuckle. Walking closer to him she whispered in his ear, "You're still cool to me."

Ken looked at the gap and put his foot over and crossed without even jumping. "It pays to be tall," he said, rubbing his short beard.

"Let's go," Daren said.

The trio jumped over several rooftops the next few hours with ease. There were luckily no twitchers up here.

Thank you God for delivering us thus far. Daren slowed his pace, his eyes frantically surveying the next rooftop.

"Everyone hold on." Daren got low to the ground as Eline and Ken walked quietly beside him. "Do you guys see that?"

The trio's eyes peered over the small chimney to see two twitchers walking on the next roof slowly.

"We need to draw their attention some way," Ken said. "Or get close for the kill."

"I could try to take them out with my crossbow," Eline offered.

"We need to try to conserve ammo. What if we get swarmed?" Daren shook his head before checking to the left and to the right.

Eline softly mused eyes lifted up to the moon, "There's a chance that the impact could ruin the arrow...or I could be able to reuse it!" She frowned, lowering her eyes back to gaze into the faces of the two men she was with. "Though I'd rather not try to creep by those things. One wrong move could be all over." She gestured behind them where the twitchers were still meandering jerkily. "We still don't know what they are truly capable of. They could see clearer at night."

"There is a possibility those things could be more inactive at night," Ken countered. "We won't know unless we try. Trial and error you know."

"An error could lead to our death," Daren said, looking sharply at Ken. "Use your head man. This isn't a movie, you know?"

"I know man. I'm playing with you." Ken elbowed him lightly to try and dissolve the tension. "Gotta keep it airy you know." His smile dropping, Ken turned his sight onto the next roof, "Enough talk, follow me." He jumped over to the next rooftop.

"Ken!" Daren looked on panicked. He quickly forced himself to calm and muttered. "Ah shoot! Come on, Eline."

Eline and Daren jumped over the three-foot gap following Ken who was walking in the darkness along the edge of the rooftop.

Ken looked back waving his hand as he walked quietly around the back corner of the roof. Eline and Daren followed two feet behind him as they rounded the corner near the chimney.

Slam! Boom!

Eline covered her mouth trying not to scream.

"You won't get me you fuckers!" a man yelled emerging onto the roof. He was walking backwards, gun drawn followed by at least nine or ten twitchers. The light from the stairwell cut a path from the door to the edge of the roof. As the man backed up he followed it unconsciously.

Boom! Boom!

"Stay down! Those are shotgun blasts," Ken said quietly. He looked through the slit in the wall as he saw the man run towards the edge of the rooftop followed by the ten twitchers.

Boom! Click, click...

"I guess I'm out," the man said, throwing the shotgun at the crazed mass before him. The man's bravo lessing as he realized his choices.

Eline and Daren peered through the slit as the man jumped off roof top with several twitchers in tow. "Wai-" Eline tried to call out but Ken put his hand over her lips quickly to silence her. Once he was gone, Ken released her mouth.

Eline turned toward Daren, shaking her head. "That poor man… "she sighed before leaning against the red brick wall "That was close."

Daren frowned, he froze, he couldn't do anything for that man…*God forgive me...*

Ken let out a heavy sigh. "Poor bastard. There are still two of those things left out there. We can take them. There is an empty shotgun over there as well. That is worth getting."

Daren looked at Ken and felt fear swell up inside of him. *I'm not fit to be a leader. I'm training to be a minister. The streets make you tough, but this is pure evil.*

Daren put his hands on his head and shook back and forth.

"You alright Daren?" Ken looked down at him. "You look out of sorts man. You got to pull it together." Ken bent down and leaned in toward his ear. "Eline is depending on you. If you don't take her, I will. Free game man. Man up brother, or step aside."

Daren didn't move. *God, I can't do it man. I can't let my heart feel as if it is about to explode. I am taking on too much. I need to wait for help. We have been lucky so far. What if a swarm comes at us?*

Eline looked over at Daren with a forced smile. "We need that shotgun, Daren. I need you to have my back. We don't want to draw attention with Ken's gun. As we say in my country 'Rise Up or Get Put Down.'" Eline leaned down to Daren's ear. "Be my hero," she said with sincerity.

Daren's eyes opened wide, and he felt fear and kindness all the same time. He nodded, standing up holding his bat.

"You ready to do this, Daren?" Ken looked at him with concern. "I will only fire if you guys get in a tight spot. I will be on the corner ready to shoot."

Daren nodded as he put his backpack down and gripped his bat. “Let's go.”

Eline walked around the corner with Daren at her back. Her eyes traced the moon and back down towards the twitcher with torn clothes.

“You okay Eline?” Daren was right on her back, nearly touching as they stepped into the moonlight.

“Yeah, stay with me okay?” Eline whispered.

“You bet,” Daren whispered.

Eline pointed her crossbow as she stopped for a moment, closing her eyes in prayer.

Eline pulled the trigger.

Swoosh!

The arrow slammed into the head of the crazed human. The empty husk fell to the ground with a smack. The second twitcher snarled, running violently towards his fallen kin.

Eline quickly pulled an arrow out of her quiver loading it into her crossbow. Taking a breath she was about to release it.

Slam! The rooftop door swung open.

“Damn they almost got me man.” A man in a torn white shirt gripped as he came onto the roof holding a pistol. Turning he noticed Eline, “A girl and one of those things. Drop it girl!” He commanded.

Eline pulled her trigger. *Swoosh!* Her arrow went through the arm of the twitcher.

The man pulled the trigger of his pistol pointing it at Eline.

Boom!

"Eline!" Daren tackled her to the ground as he felt two bullets zoom over their heads.

Boom! Boom! Boom! Three shots rang out.

Daren looked up as he saw Ken appear from behind the corner.

The man and the twitcher remained motionless on the rooftop. The moonlight was their only solace as silence once more descended on the night.

Chapter 6

June 2nd, 2015

Aegis City – 42nd Street Downtown

3:15 A.M

Ken ran over to them, helping up Eline and Daren. "You guys good?" A bubble of panic colored his words.

Daren stared at Ken. "We owe you our lives," he said gratefully. *Greater love has no one than this: to lay down one's life for one's friends. John 15:13. Though, why am I thinking of that verse? Ken's still very much alive…*

"Yeah. We are good." Eline ran over to the edge of the roof grabbing the shotgun.

A crackly voice came from where the man's body lay. "Okay, okay are you there?"

The trio froze in place at the sudden intrusion.

Ken turned around, looking at the body on the roof. The crackling voice came again. "Are you there, man? Did you clear the roof? We are heading up in a minute."

Eline's eyes looked frantically at Daren and Ken as if they were reading each other's minds. Daren and Ken ran over to the body and started to search. Ken grabbed the radio receiver and pulled up the man's single remaining sleeve. "Oh man." he gasped, dropping the material.

Daren looked down, and tugged the material up himself to see a tattoo with two claws intersecting under the fabric. "We killed a gang member. He was a member of the Central City Wolverines." Daren mechanically filled in.

"I thought they were losing ground to the other kingpins, but they seem to be operating to some extent," Ken said.

Eline ran over holding her crossbow and the shotgun over her shoulder. "You should have this, Daren." She offered the empty shotgun to him.

Daren stared at the shotgun, his brain trying to catch up and comprehend all the information that was around him…gang member dead, shotgun, radio, coming up soon. His eyes snapped open wider! Grabbing the shotgun from her offered hand he barked, "Let's move now!" Daren ran toward the edge of the next roof, this one about four feet in length.

"Ugh!" Daren landed hard, scraping his knee on the pavement. Ken and Eline barely crossed the gap as they got behind the air conditioner fan mounted there.

Ken clicked off the radio as the trio looked over the fan cautiously.

It was hard to clearly see the entire roof from where they hid. Moments turned to minutes and minutes seemed like hours. A clearly angered, deep, male voice yelled, "Who did this?"

Other figures moved to become more visible. Daren started to mentally count the amount of men in the group he could see. "There are at least ten people over there," Daren said.

"Two dead of these crazy things," a tall man said, kicking at one of the twitcheer's lifeless bodies. Pulling out the arrow from one of the twitcher's arms that man presented it to another that was hard to see.

Another voice shouted, "Hey Gery was shot!"

"Not Gery!"

"Let's get his body down."

A man with long dreadlocks walked out amongst the crowd of armed men. "Those sons of bitches are going to pay" the man growled, his voice boiling with unreleased rage. Blowing smoke out of his cigarette the man moved further into their line of vision to toss the used bud off the roof top to the ground below.

Daren's eyes looked in horror as the lastest man with the cigarette looked hauntingly familiar. It was his cousin Michael that stood before him.

Ken watched the situation trying to stay calm. "We have to go… Daren?" He gazed to where his friend and neighbor was sitting, shaking but unresponsive. "Daren!" he hissed.

Eline looked over at Daren who was shaking violently. She put her hand on his shoulder. "Daren?" she questioned. Closing her eyes she quoted "Be strong and courageous, Do not be afraid; do not be discouraged, for the Lord your God will be with you wherever you go." She looked in his eyes "Joshua 1:9. I recite that verse a lot being so far from home."

Ken frowned, "What good does all of that do?" he quietly spat. You're wasting time!

Glancing up, she nodded. Her eyes narrowed as she understood time was of the essence, "We need to move you guys." She agreed, padding Daren on the shoulder she rose.

Daren took a shaky breath. The verse was comforting and was helping him to refocus and calm down. Getting up carefully he went to turn around as a large man with light skin stood before him.

"We got some runts over here," the large man yelled across the rooftop to his team.

"Time to go!" Ken said, pointing his revolver at the man's lower body. *Boom!* The man fell to one knee, fuming in anger. "They're getting AWAY!!!" he screamed.

Daren took his bat and slammed it into the man's face, knocking him out. "Run!" Daren yelled.

The trio sprinted across the rooftops. The bullets whizzed by their heads ricocheting off of bricks and other metal objects.

Eline screamed, falling to the ground.

"Eline!" Daren turned around, lifting her arm around his shoulder and guiding her toward the stairs that were ten feet away. "You will not fear the terror of night, nor the arrow that flies by day…" he muttered to himself as he ran. "... A thousand may fall at your side, ten thousand at your right hand, but it will not come near you…[2]" *We are getting out of this… we are getting out of this!*

Ken ran in front of them as the yelling faded.

Eline and Daren hobbled down the stairs reaching Ken who was trying to kick in the door.

"Shoot! If anyone is there, open up. Please," Ken pleaded, leaning on the door.

A faint voice was on the other side. "Drop your weapons and I will open up."

"I won't but I will step back ten feet and point my weapon in the air so you can get the first shot." Ken stepped back and to his surprise the door clicked open.

A muscular man stood in front of Ken. "Come in but keep that weapon pointed at the sky" the man gave him a stern look before sliding his eyes over to Eline and Daren. "Come on in…I'm not worried about you two. I can take you." He pointed over at Ken. "It's the sly one here I am worried about. He's quite good with words."

The man stepped back as the trio entered the building. The large man closed the heavy door behind them. He locked the door with a deadbolt lock, and put a door stop on it.

"You guys can drop the gun, especially you playboy. Plus, you're empty."

Ken let out a small laugh.

"You can push back the freezer," the mysterious man said to Ken. Then turning to Eline and Daren. "You two can come with me." The large man walked through the doors into a kitchen area which led into what appeared to be a record store.

Daren continued to help Eline walk as it was apparent she was limping. He looked at the wall as he saw the initial C.C.

It can't be… "Are you Curtis Chop?"

The muscular man laughed. "You guessed it…"

Daren and Eline followed the large man past the record store area into a large office.

"You guys can put your weapons down right there," Curtis said in a deep voice.

Daren laid down his equipment and then took Elines to help her lay hers down. He went back to help Eline stand both of them silently looking at their host.

"Let me see the girl for a moment." He pointed to a chair. "Sit over here on the reclining sofa and pull up your leggings."

Daren nodded and led Eline over to the large reclining chair. She winced as Daren helped her pull up her legging. Daren flashed her a small strained smile in apology.

Curtis approached and inspected the leg and ankle. "No gunshot wounds, which is good. Let me know if this hurts." Curtis pressed around on the ankle of Eline.

"Ouch… ooh" She squirmed with the sudden pain. "That spot! It's tender to the touch." Eline clinched her fist taking in a few breaths.

Curtis sighed he knew what was most likely wrong… Living where he was he'd seen his share of twisted, sprained, broken and dislocated body parts before… This one was dislocated…"This is going to hurt."

"Hurt?" Eline asked sharply. But I didn't have time to get an answer or process further.

Curtis took both of his hands and twisted Eline's ankle slightly, popping it back into place.

"Ahh!" Eline cried out and wriggled in her chair.

"That should do it," Curtis said, tapping her ankle twice. He then turned to look at Daren with a concerned look. "So, what's your name kid?"

"It's Daren," he said, holding out his hand.

"Ummm I see… and the young lady here?" Curtis asked.

The pain dulling, she was testing out her ankle by carefully moving it in circles. "I'm Eline. Thank you for taking us in."

Curtis shook both of their hands. "What about the other guy? The one with a smart mouth?"

"That's Ken. he's a bit of a playboy and goofy," Daren scratched his head.

"People like that will get you killed…" Curtis looked at them with serious intent. "You're not dead yet though so he must have some redeeming qualities." Curtis stood up, his massive figure towering over Daren. "Let me show you around really quick."

Daren waved at Eline leaving her to rest her ankle a bit more as he followed Curtis into the main area.

"You got some classics in here," Ken said, looking up at Curtis and Daren.

"If you break them, you have to pay for them," Curtis said. "The one you are holding is worth three thousand dollars. If you so choose you can put it on the record player if you dare." "Each step could lead to your pocket being destroyed once this is all over."

Ken looked down at the record, putting it back slowly into its sleeve.

Curtis let out a loud laugh as he opened the door. "You all can sleep in here. This is the accounting office but there are a few blow up mattresses here. You saw the kitchen." Curtis closed the door.

Daren looked up at the silver and gold platinum frames. *This dude is a living legend. They said he left town though to start another business. I guess he is as mysterious as they say.* "Do you miss the Tough Enough Crew?"

Curtis stopped for a moment and turned around. "I miss them. I miss Mic-T most of all. He was a good man. Now he's a shell of himself putting out crappy music. All about hoes and stuff. The music we created had meaning. I hear the stuff he puts out. It's shock value and no substance." He shook his head as if mourning a person who passed too soon from this world. "All buzz and no nectar. The music we created you can still listen to today and it's hard.

Daren followed Curtis as he saw a room with a cracked door. *He does have a golden mix table.*

Curtis turned around looking at Daren shutting the door. "Don't go getting any ideas." He pointed further down the hall. "Down there are the showers and restrooms."

Daren chuckled trying not to be intimated. *This hallway is narrow, and his shoulders are almost as wide as the hallway.*

Curtis turned around with a small smile. "Don't make me regret taking you in. Some of the young people today don't respect their elders."

Though Curtis was up in his early fifties he was in impressive shape. His bald head and neatly trimmed gray beard gave him a cool grandfather vibe that went with the records store.

"I wouldn't think of it," Daren said, putting his hands up crossing them over quickly.

Daren turned around as Curtis followed him to the office where Eline was still sitting.

Daren walked in and saw Ken leaning against the wall with his eyes closed and Eline looking up at the ceiling. "Are you doing okay, Eline?"

Eline nodded with a cheerful smile. "making it during the end of the world, you know. It's quite a feat we aren't dead yet. Jesus is guiding the way so I know all will be fine…" She let out a breath and wrapped her arms around herself.

"You guys get some sleep. The store is safe and it's soundproof because it doubles as a studio for beginning artists. Little man will guide you to where you can get some shut eye."

Little man…wow he gave me a nickname. Daren shrugged his shoulders in disbelief.

"Dang man that's cold," Ken said laughing.

"I think it's cute," Eline said, putting out her hand towards Daren.

Daren shook his head slightly. *I guess it's better than nothing I suppose. I'm not little though. I'm a grown man. Compared to him I'm tiny.*

Daren took Eline's hand and guided her and Ken to the sleeping area he saw a minute before. "We will all be bunking here in this room,"

Daren said. "He said there are three blow-up beds and it should be no problem at all if we stay a few days. I don't think we should overstay our welcome."

Ken smirked widely. "I think we should rest for a while. We have no idea what is going on in the rest of the city. We should turn that radio back on and see what's up. We also need to conserve the battery as well. It's fully charged right now. Waiting on some sort of cue or info will probably not happen."

"Daren is right. Those gangsters…" Eline paused, looking over at Daren.

Daren looked down at the ground. *I haven't even had time to process what Michael did up there with those guys. He's their leader. No wonder he's been gone so long. He only reached out in text and never called. Even so he was always there for me.... he's family.*

"We can talk about all of this after we rest." Ken walked into the room putting down his equipment and sat down on one of the mattresses stretching out.

"Daren, I think I can walk a little bit on my own." Eline looked over to him with a cheerful smile. Eline walked gingerly towards the women's showers down the hallway.

"Oh Daren, come here for a moment."

Daren, looking away into the distance, walked over to Eline who was in front of the women's door.

"Thank you for coming back to pick me up when I fell." Eline leaned in and gave a gentle kiss to his right ear. "You're a brave person, silly. Thank God I found you." As she leaned in and pressed herself against him in a hug. Her small arms encircling his back and rubbing it slightly.

Daren's cheeks flared up trying to find the words in his mouth. His arms reciprocating and encircling her as well. He had felt like he was in hell, but with these simple sweet actions, he felt like he was getting a taste of heaven. "Ah…ahh…You're welcome Eline," he said, releasing her and blushing stumbled off quickly towards the men's shower.

Daren turned back to see Eline looking at him with a glowing smile. Daren blushed pushing the door toward the men shower.

I didn't expect that…oh man…I haven't felt emotions like that since my first kiss in high school. She kissed my ear and for a moment tenderly sucked on it. That is a bit much.

Daren jumped in the shower soaking his face underneath the hot water. Letting the normalcy of the task wash over him. Finally, he could take some time to reflect. *God so much has happened in the past two days. I killed someone... I felt their blood on my hand…. I set others up to die too… I even stood by and LET people DIE!* Daren looked at his hands and started to scrub them more trying to wash them clean. Flashes of the crazed woman he killed, the men they ran from that were chasing them in the hallway, the mother and child in the streets, the men on the rooftop all flashed in his mind. It had been numb but now he felt dirty and wanted to be sick. The blood that had been everywhere as they walked out of his door… He recalled the screams and pleas of the woman outside his door before some psycho-- no -- no a scared, lost child of God murdered her. *He felt his stomach flipping and his heart ached. This isn't ME! I'm here to evangelize to save people! I'm such a screw up!* He banged his fist several times on the tile of the shower shaking. Tears started to fall from his eyes and mix with the shower water. His body wracked with sobs that he quieted.

He was the leader. He had to be strong… *But what if I CAN'T be that strong?! Jesus! I can't do it! I can't! I can't! "I CAN'T!"* He verbalized his thoughts, his voice gravely and rough filled with the hopelessness he had been shoving back. The hopelessness of the situation before him.

Taking a shaky breath, the water was still raining on his back and head, dripping off his nose, chin and body. His thoughts weren't done with him yet. *My cousin is a gang leader. I'm going to the location he suggested but I don't even know if it's truly safe or what I'll say when I see him! Oh, Oh! And the world is coming to an end!* His wild thoughts paused for a heartbeat. *Where ARE you Jesus? Why are you letting this happen? I need your peace over me... I need your love. Most of all I need your protection. We don't know how long this is going to be. Am I going to die? Am I doing what is right? Why am I having to go through this?*

Daren stood there for a long time, sobbing, hunched over in the shower. When he had cried all he could he stood there breathing. That's when a new set of thoughts started to populate his mind. *I'm in a warm shower…. I'm alive… I saved Eline… I MET Eline because of this.* Lifting a hand he gingerly brought it to his ear. He remembered her soft lips and the heartbeat she had dared to give that bold little pull with her mouth on it before hugging him… He took a deep breath, felt himself calm and gain confidence. Daren ran his hands through his hair, the shampoo rushing down his body as he stood there. His tears had finally dried. God, I know I made mistakes. I don't know what I'm doing… This is terrifying. But look where I am. *I can do it! I know I can! God has too much left for me to do. I'm sorry for what I did, and I don't know what to do. So God, guide me...*

Daren turned the water and stepped out of the shower. Grabbing a towel, he looked at a small toothbrush and toothpaste that was unopened. *It's like he planned on taking in survivors even though he didn't mention it. I need some sleep.*

Daren brushed his teeth and turned off the light to the bathroom. *I guess I will sleep in my boxers.*

Daren walked toward the room, Eline and Ken were already knocked out and snoring. His eyes traced the room. Some records were neatly stacked in the corner and the walls were painted a brown color.

That brown reminds me of my grandpa's old classic car. That sound was lovely. Daren walked over to the mattress in the corner slowly trying not to wake up his sleeping friends. Oddly, a smile graced his face as he made it to his mattress in the top right of the room.

God, thank you for bringing me this far.

Daren laid down on the floor, his mind drifting slowly into dream land.

"Hey…hey, wake up Daren."

Daren shook his head as he felt a soft hand on his forehead.

"Wake up silly," Eline said. "It's time for breakfast."

Daren stood up, looking into Eline's eyes.

"You are the last one to wake up. We didn't want your food to get cold," she said, jumping up into the air.

"God woke us up for another day. We've got to keep the joy going." Eline twirled in a circle near the door.

She is so cheerful in spite of it all. God how does she - the joy of the Lord is your strength[3] *That verse fits her but what does it even truly mean?* Daren looked down at his cellphone. *11:45…It's a bit late for breakfast.* He looked over his mattress down a neatly folded stack of clothes. *Who did my laundry?*

Daren stood up putting on his clothes. He walked out the door and to the kitchen to see everyone standing around a long metal cooking table.

"About time you woke up," Curtis said. "My dad used to wake me up at six AM to start our morning jog. No days off… I heard that more than I would have liked. It instilled a work ethic in me that only kept me alive but put me ahead of my peers. You young people could learn a thing from us. Maybe your life would be a lot better."

Daren looked away for a moment but knew Curtis was right.

"I will let it slide this time," Curtis said, handing him a plate. "Your friend filled me in on what happened. You are kind of the leader of this band. You should bulk up a bit you know."

Daren was too tired to respond. "I let my fitness go a bit while I was in college. None of that matters now since the world is ending."

"We don't know that," Curtis countered.

"For all we know the military could be clearing out the whole town and it's a matter of time." Ken looked at the trio with a small smile.

"They don't care about us," Curtis said. "I could make a lot more money in the uptown, but I wanted to be amongst my people. We are low hanging fruit. If those rich people wanted to, they could clear out this whole area and make another mall or something."

"Tell us how you really feel." Ken teased as he took another bite of his bacon.

"We can talk about that later," Daren interjected. "Last night before bed I was thinking about our current inventory."

“We made it this far by God’s grace,” Eline said, patting him on the back.

Ken rolled his eyes at Eline’s nieveness. “A little luck too,” Ken added.

Curtis put some eggs, pancakes, bacon and a slice of toast on Daren’s plate

“Thank you,” Daren said, leaning on the cold metal. Turning his mind back to business. “We have a shotgun, one revolver, one pistol, a bat, trash can lid, medical supplies, and a few other things. I think we are traveling a bit too heavy. We need to figure out what we need. We need to travel light.”

“It sounds like you are serious about getting out of town.” Curtis glanced at Daren with a concerning look. “Why the rush? You could wait it out.”

“We have no idea what those things are capable of,” Eline piped up with intensity before picking up a piece of her bacon to nibble on.

Ken crossed his arms slowly. “I'd rather not wait around because what if a bunch of them slam into your door or something.

“That is why I have blackout curtains and this store is soundproof for the most part. I could stay here for a while. I have enough food for a few weeks.” He eyed the younger group firmly. They seemed foolish, but maybe this piece of the puzzle would help them understand, “I did hear something on the radio some hours ago. The military and police were targeted. It would appear this is an act of terrorism. Something or someone unleashed something at each corner of the city thus spreading it throughout the whole city.”

"We don't know if we have been infected already or not?" Eline put out her hands, waving them wildly in disgust-- ironically twitching as a twitcher might. "I could already have it and turn into one of those things without notice."

"That's a possibility based on what we heard," Ken said. A confident smirk crossed his face as he leaned towards Eline and stated smoothly, "You would make for a pretty twitcher I guess."

Daren elbowed Ken in the shoulder. "Come on man, that's not cool."

"I'm trying to keep it light," Ken shrugged his shoulders.

Eline shook her head looking at the table. "Essentially, we know nothing. I don't want to wait around to die. Those things are everywhere. We could be infected, dormant, or immune. I guess it's like roulette."

"Sounds like it," Curtis said.

Daren suddenly remembered yet another blessing. "Oh, Curtis, thank you for doing our laundry. Our clothes were filthy after sweating so much."

Curtis smiled for one moment and went back to making some more bacon. "No problem little man. There are times when artists have to stay the night, so I invested in the necessary items to make my studio feel at home."

"Thank you," the trio said, chomping down on their breakfast.

"Let's rest up and move out tonight. How is your ankle Eline?"

"It's okay. A little sore but I can walk on it. Honestly, another day of rest would be helpful. I'm shaken up like you. I don't want to slow anyone down."

Ken nodded his head. "I agree… I think we should rest. I'm all about pressing forward but what's the point if we are not at hundred percent." That flirtatious smirk was back as he looked at the girl with them. "I would have to look after Eline or carry her if her ankle goes out."

"Ahhh, as if Ken..." Eline giggled looking over at Daren with a big smile. Her eyes landed on his arms as if remembering when he helped her the night before.

Her look made Daren shiver a moment. As his mind traveled back to the kiss and hug last night… *Oh Lord!*

"You're welcome to stay here as long as you want," Curtis said. "But you make a fair point. Anything could happen to the city. It only took a day for everything to fall apart. With lack of response my conclusion is that there was a bioterrorism attack on the military and police. We have to fend for ourselves."

The truth washed over the four of them as if a close friend died.

Daren clinched his fist as he tried to focus on the task at hand.

"Everything is going to be okay?" Eline asked, looking at him with concern.

Boom! Boom!

Ken turned to the large door at the end of the kitchen.

Curtis walked over to the fridge putting his hand on his sawed-off shotgun.

Daren clinched the knife he was holding while cutting his pancakes.

Curtis walked slowly toward the large steel door. Leaning his head against the door, he heard a faint growl.

Walking back to the table he put the shotgun back at its location. "It was one of those twisted humans. I heard the growl through the steel."

Eline let out a sigh as she sipped her coffee.

Ken looked at Curtis with a reassuring smile. "Thanks for checking on that. I'm a bit shaken up too."

"After what you guys went through last night you should rest up. Here are some leftovers," Curtis said as he started to clean up his grill.

"Do you think it was drawn to the smell of cooked meat?" Eline asked.

"Maybe if that was the case a lot more would have shown up. That thing was wandering the back-alley ways and slammed into the door."

Daren looked at his two friends and smiled. "Let's relax today y'all." Daren turned around, heading out of the room towards the artist lounge.

"Ken, I took care of that thing you wanted," Curtis said, not looking back at him while he cleaned the griddle.

Ken nodded as he stood up and walked out of the room toward the record store area.

Eline looked curiously at Ken as he left. *I wonder what that was about?*

"Don't push yourself too hard, Eline," Curtis turned around with a dirty spatula. "You say your leg is well, but I have seen injuries like that when I used to work for Aegis PD. That's a pretty serious swell."

Eline smiled. "You know your injuries. We call these horse knots where I come from."

"Your accent is lovely," Curtis said. "It reminds me of a lost love from long ago across the sea." Curtis walked toward the sink cleaning his spatula. "That young man cares about you deeply. He's a good kid. I see him working hard talking to people on the streets and taking care of schoolwork. He used to come in here a lot, but I was always mixing. I saw him from the camera. His parents a few years ago were in a bombing in uptown. It was the worst attack the city had seen in a long time."

Eline twirled her pigtails as she stared deeply at Curtis.

"If you care for him, then let him know." Curtis' deep voice softened slightly. "That was a mistake I made long ago. I didn't return the love I was given. I was a fool. In this current state, who knows where love may come from."

Eline felt her heart beat faster. She nodded, starting to walk off to contemplate what was told to her.

"Thinking is a good young one." He called, stopping her in her tracks. "Overthinking can lead to doubt. Some things are as simple as they seem." Curtis finished washing his spatula laying it neatly on the dish mat.

Eline turned and noticed the mess. She went back and picked up the plates, scraping the extra food into the nearby trash can.

"Thanks for helping to clean up. You have a good head on your shoulders," Curtis said.

"My papa and mama raised me to clean up. Also, if we didn't clean-up, we would not be able to play. It's part of our culture." Eline filled the sink with bubbles and scrubbed the dishes with warm water.

Eline felt a buzz in her pocket. *What?*

Drying her hands quickly she pulled out her phone as she read the text. *Franklin is dead… He protected us to the very end in the church. Many people turned into those crazy things and only my daughter and a few others survived. I found the pastor's phone in his office and wanted to let you know. Do not go to your church. Be safe and may God guide us all.—- Pastor Kenneth Smith.*

Eline felt her body lean to the left slowly as she steadied herself. "Franklin!"

"You okay young one?" Curtis asked.

"Yeah… yeah got some bad news," Eline said, trying to hold back tears. "Thank you for breakfast." she squeaked out her voice gaining pitch with her sorrow. Eline walked slowly out of the room towards the resting area. "God… I can't take this… where are you?" she whispered a small prayer to herself.

Eline opened the door to see Daren sitting down on the mattress reading a history novel.

"Yo!" Daren put his hand up in greeting. Noticing Eline's face, the smile he wore faded. "What's wrong?"

Eline walked mechanically over to him and plopped down beside him before wrapping her arms around him. Her eyes let go of a few tears as she sniffled and sobbed.

"Let me put my book away first…" he trailed, setting it open on the other side of him. "What wrong?" he asked again, wrapping his arms around her.

"I don't want to lose you…Daren."

"Dying is not my agenda," Daren said, letting out a small smile.

"Franklin is dead, Daren. He's dead… I got a text from Pastor Kenneth. Franklin died protecting people. He's dead… I didn't even get to see him one last time. Gone… gone… my mentor and someone who means so much to me."

Eline sobbed her tears wetting Daren's shoulder.

Daren held Eline close for a while until her breath steadied.

"Pastor Franklin was a kind man. He is relaxing in heaven now walking with Jesus. No more pain as the good word says." Daren tried not to blush looking at Eline's tear filled gaze.

Eline looked up at Daren's face an inch away from his. "You know, Daren, I am as afraid as you are."

Daren felt Eline's breath… It was still sweet with syrup from the pancakes from breakfast. *Don't kiss her, you've only known her for a day. It would be wrong of me to take advantage of her in a time of weakness.*

Eline closed her eyes as the tears continued to flow out of her eyes. Leaning her head back, her lips puckered, seeming to be waiting.

"His death wasn't in vain… Pastor Franklin will be hailed a hero." Daren hugged Eline again. He leaned into her hair.

Eline cheeks flared up as she sighed. "Men…" she muttered flustered.

Daren let go of Eline and he smiled at her. "You should rest your leg. We have a long journey ahead of us."

"It is okay if I stay with you a little bit." Eline twirled her pigtails looking down at Daren who was spread out on his mattress.

"Sure," Daren spoke softly, moving over to let Eline lay beside him.

"Thank you, silly. I appreciate you," Eline said with a soft giggle. It wasn't her usual flare but she was able to at least smile a little bit.

Daren felt Eline wrap her arms around him as he closed his eyes to rest after a hearty breakfast.

Ken stood from the comfy massage chair. The love birds had been resting for several hours now. It was good for them to rest. He had no idea what Curtis was up to. However, he had been nowhere in sight. Perhaps he was resting too... "Since he is away, I can take a look…" he muttered looking around carefully to confirm he wouldn't get caught. Ken walked out of the kitchen through the guest area towards the forbidden mixing room. "It's all mine baby." he whispered, rubbing his hands together in glee.

Ken's eyes traced the golden record table with happy eyes. "I remember seeing this in the video when I was a kid." He walked around it. His eyes took it in reverently. "The golden mix table is one of the most coveted items of the hip hop era." Ken went out to touch the golden turntable. "How much did this thing cost?" he mused fingers a hair away from actually touching it.

"Too much for your hand to handle that's for sure," Curtis said entering the room.

"Oh!" Ken jumped into the air almost falling to the ground.

"It's alright man I get it," Curtis said, putting out his hand to Ken. "I also said not to come in here. I could body slam your behind right now."

As nice as Curtis was being about this, the set of the man's shoulders and eyes showed he meant what he said. Also Curtis was a big guy…. it would hurt. "I don't think a body slam would be the best thing for me." Ken answered conversationally, growing more uncomfortable by the moment. His words gained a higher pitch and speed as he continued. "Especially-since- the-world-is-currently-falling-apart." Ken stood, shaking trying to hold his composure.

"You sure you don't want a body slam. It may teach you some manners." Curtis let go a small smile looking at Ken on the ground shaking slightly.

"I'm good man… you shouldn't scare a brother like that." Ken stood, brushing off his clothes trying to seem unaffected by the massive man standing in front of him.

"You know man I will give you a taste of what this thing is maybe before you leave," Curtis said. "Maybe. Now see your way out of my mixing room. I shouldn't have to lock my own door. I will let you slide this time because of curiosity."

Ken walked slowly past Curtis trying not to look at him.

Curtis looked down at Ken smirking slightly. "Next time it's a body slam," he said, smacking Ken on the back lightly.

Ken straightened up at the minor spike of pain before he walked out the room as he heard Curtis go in and turn on the music slightly. Seeing the door close behind him Ken sighed looking at it longingly. "He could have let me see a little bit of his work. Maybe he is working on something new. Something inspired by the end of the world." He dropped his shoulders a bit disappointed, "I guess I can respect that."

Ken walked into the main area of the record store looking for one of his favorite records as a child.

In the makeshift guest room, Daren rolled over to see Eline with a smile curled up beside him.

God is this real… A woman coming onto me like this. I don't want to take advantage of the situation. She is fine… I mean fine, Jesus.

Daren stood up slowly as he glanced at his phone.

It's already 5:30. I guess I was more tired than I realized.

Daren went to the kitchen to fetch the radio he got from the laptop. *Michael, what are you doing man? I thought better of you cousin. There has to be a reason. He could have been… what? held captive - no maybe there is another explanation?* Daren ran a hand through his hair. *There is no need to gangbang. You can be more… that money… money can be an evil thing when used the wrong way.*

Daren clicked on the radio. It showed max battery. *I need to conserve this as much as possible.*

A male voice came over the radio singing a song. "Hoes, cash, money, get it in. Make that thing pop."

Daren clicked off the radio as he shook his head. *Is that what all these dudes think about? Getting women? They have to be doing* more. *They were clearing buildings when we found them on that rooftop. If they are clearing each building, then they will eventually get here. Curtis Chop is an influential figure of the city. Hopefully, they will not touch him.*

Daren looked over to find Eline standing in the walkway smiling softly. *She's quite lovely.*

Daren started to walk towards Eline. He was drawn to her. As he opened his mouth to say something he felt a rumble and the building around them started to shake.

"What is that?" Daren raced towards the window as he eyes widened. "Everyone run!" Daren screamed at the top of his lungs. *Plane getting bigger! Not good! Not good!* Daren ran towards Eline as quickly as he could. The noise got deafening as Daren tackled Eline to the ground covering her head.

BOOM! Smoke and debris blocked all vision in what was left of the building. The sound defining.

Chapter 7

June 2nd 2015

Aegis City – 52nd Street, Downtown

7 pm

Daren coughed as dust covered his skin. A ringing in his ears. He looked down at Eline who was shaking in fear

Eline was saying something, but he couldn't hear her. Her lips were moving but he couldn't hear... "What?" he called loudly. He felt the sound shift to quiet more until it was all but gone.

"Thank you for covering me, Daren." She quickly kissed him on the lips smiling but was still shaking.

Daren blushed as he stood up and brushed off the ceiling rubble that fell on them.

"Is everyone okay?" Curtis asked, running into the main room.

"Yeah, yeah we are good," Eline and Daren yelled back.

Ken ran in, his voice high pitched and his disposition as a ghost. "This isn't good guys. I was taking a smoke on the other side of the alleyway. A plane crashed and took out the roof and people were falling out. Oh my God…some of them were turning into things. We have to go. It crashed two blocks away."

Daren stood up dusting off his shirt. He put his hand out to help Eline.

"Thank you," Eline said kindly, taking his hand.

"Everyone get your stuff," Curtis said. "We need to leave. This place isn't safe."

Daren ran to the kitchen, finding his backpack. *I need to take the shotgun and bat. Travel light.*

He looked at the shotgun, it felt heavier. *There is ammo in this gun… maybe...*

Eline stood behind him, putting the trash can lid on her back. She looked over to Daren who was holding the shotgun tightly. "It's going to be okay Daren." Eline put her hand on his hand as she turned to run through the rubble back toward the main record store area.

Daren stood there for a moment looking at the dark gray walls of the kitchen. *God keep us safe. This is getting crazy. The past two days of life have been nothing but my worst nightmare. I am surprised I haven't passed out or lost it mentally. I feel as if my whole world is falling apart. What do I do if I find my cousin? I can't shoot him… he's blood.*

Daren gripped his baseball bat as he turned and ran towards the main area.

"You guys ready?" Curtis asked, walking in with two and large size revolvers and on his back a sawed-off shotgun.

The trio nodded, following Curtis out the side door of the studio. The smelling of burning fuel penetrated their nostrils from miles away.

"Do you think there are any survivors?" Eline looked up to the others as she checked surroundings behind her.

"Probably not," Curtis said in a low voice.

"If there are, they may be turned into those things." Ken added darkly.

Curtis led the ground down toward a back alleyway which was lined by stairs and children's toys.

Daren looked back at Eline who was turning in a 360-motion checking their rear and ensuring they were not ambushed. "You're doing great, you know," Daren said quietly to her trying not to laugh or show too much emotion.

Eline blushed, her pigtails blowing in the light wind that was traveling down the alleyway. "Thank you."

"Hold fast everyone," Curtis said as they came up to a car garage on their right. "My ride is up there. We have to cross the street to get there."

Curtis looked up at the roof of the buildings and back toward the ground. "I noticed some windows open but nothing out of the ordinary. The plane landed about three blocks to the west so that route is blocked off. The whole block is on fire."

"Do you guys hear that?" Daren looked up at the sky and around back to the start of the alley way.

"Yeah, I hear it too," Ken said with a somber face.

The sirens got louder as a fire truck barreled past them speeding down towards the flames of the plane wreckage.

"Those idiots," Ken said, trying not to yell.

"We have to go now," Curtis said.

The group of four sprinted across the road as the sight to their revealed the horror that was about to unload.

"Ah shit!" Ken yelled.

Out of their corner of their eyes the group saw what appeared to be a horde of twitchers running full sprint after the fire truck.

"Keep going!" Curtis yelled as he ran up the ramp past the customer post of the parking garage. "I am on the second floor. Double time it, people."

Eline looked back panting for breath as her worst fears came to fruition. Her voice shrieked as she saw not five, but ten twitchers branch off from the large horde that was chasing the fire truck. "Guys we got ten of those things following us."

Curtis, Daren, and Ken looked back.

"Those things don't run out of energy, we have to shoot back," Daren said.

"Can we make it up the ramp without them catching us?" Ken turned around holding his revolver.

Boom!

The bullet pierced the first twitcher in the head, dropping it instantly.

"Nice shot Ken!" Daren looked over at him with a smile. Daren's wide smile turned to dismay as if the whole world slowed down around him. Before the words could leave his mouth, a twitcher tackled Ken to the ground.

"Agh!" Ken yelled in anguish as he felt the twitcher stop moving as an arrow pierced the head of the twitcher.

"Ken!" Eline ran up to see a massive scratch on his arm.

"There is no time! You guys have to go take my weapons and go. Those things are coming." Ken sat up.

Curtis clenched his fist as he turned around. "Kid, I'm sorry. Everyone, we have to keep going. My SUV is up around the corner."

Daren looked down at Ken who was trying not to tear up. "Your God has you, my brother." Daren put his hand on his shoulder. He knew what was going to happen to him….

Eline's eyes were red as she bent down touching Ken's head with hers. "I'm sorry Ken. I'm so sorry." Eline stood, running with Daren as they followed Curtis up the steep incline towards the second floor of the parking garage.

"Y'all muthafuckers think you can take me!" he yelled. Ken put his backpack down, opening it quickly. *It's been a while since I used these.*

Ken took out two brass knuckles with spikes on them and a golden robe that said Kenny "The Bull" Mathers in black letters. Kenny felt his right arm twitch as he stood. "Prepare to face the underground boxing champion!" Ken ran toward the mob as fast as he could, delivering a right hook shattering the chin of the first twitcher. Quickly running to the left, he delivered an uppercut breaking the jaw of the second crazed individual. The blood from the two crazed humans covered the spikes of the brass knuckles.

Ken felt his left arm go numb as he clenched his fist. Luckily muscle memory for a boxer makes them immune to numbness.

Before he knew it one of the twitchers tackled him. Clenching his fist, Ken drove his brass knuckles into the skull of the husk shattering its skull. "I will not give up!" He roared. The sound echoing in the garage.

"Poor Ken!" Eline's voice cracked as she ran toward Daren who was rounding the next corner of the slope with Curtis.

Curtis looked back at Eline with a look of sincerity. "All we can do is survive," he said in a deep voice. "There is my ride right there."

Daren looked forward at a black SUV with big wheels and dark tinted windows.

Curtis ran towards the driver side door jumping in and starting the car. Eline jumped in the back seat and Daren in the front seat.

"Welcome Curtis Chop." a friendly female voice said.

"Voice activation off," Curtis said hurriedly, turning on the SUV.

"Everyone seatbelts on if you can! Here we go!" Curtis pressed on the gas turning to the right towards the bottom heading to the exit of the garage.

The SUV turned sharply despite its size as Curtis slammed on the brakes.

The trio's eyes traced Ken standing with his back to the SUV and his fist raised in the air. Blood covered his golden robe and knuckles. A mass of dead twicher bodies encircling his form. All their hearts thundered watching.

"Oh God…" Eline breathed hands folded in prayer.

Ken turned around slowly, his body shaking violently. His eyes were already a white color, but he made no movement to lunge towards the SUV.

Eline swallowed and leaned up tapping Curtis on the shoulder. Then she pointed towards the sunroof.

Curtis solemnly nodded, opening the sunroof with the golden button on the navigation.

Eline perched on the top of the window pointing her crossbow towards the head of Ken. "Goodbye my friend. You were on fire." Eline pressed the trigger as the bow traveled quickly penetrating the skull of their comrade.

Eline got back into the car sitting down into the seat trying not to cry. Daren looked back at her. He put his hand on her knee and rubbed it gently. Eline put her hand on his, holding it for a moment. "The Lord is close to the brokenhearted…" Daren quoted maybe that was why he got that verse yesterday morning.

Curtis pressed the gas slightly as they drove past Ken's body which was motionless on the pavement.

Smoke filled the air as Curtis pulled up to the intersection.

"You said your aunt's place is to the west toward the new extension?" Curtis looked over at Daren with a concerned look.

"It could be cluttered with cars or blocked with twitchers." Daren looked to the left and to the right.

"You sure that's the best thing little man. I think we should head to the south side and see if it's less cluttered," Curtis commented, gripping the wheel. "From what Ken said, you haven't seen this auntie in years. We could be doing the wrong thing honestly and I am the one behind the wheel."

"Look man, if you don't want to help us you don't have to. I understand that it's crazy out here and you have your own interest."

"My interest will probably go up in flames…" Curtis looks to the right as his studio was broken because of the plane crash.

Daren looked back at Eline who was smiling, shaking her head up and down.

"Curtis, we need you man. You took care of us and helped Eline with her injury. There is someone I need to talk to as well that hurts me deeply. There is unfinished business in the city I have."

"Way to show your resolve, little man. I get it… you have things to settle. I can't leave a brother out there to dry." Curtis smiled a bit trying to be funny, "Are you a child of God? Why don't you ask Jesus where we are supposed to go. He's all knowing right? Heck ask him to end all of this if he's even real."

"Don't mock Christ like that," Eline said, smacking him on the shoulder.

Curtis let go another small smile as he turned right heading past his record store and up the hill towards a smaller road.

Daren looked out the window at the moon and it was beautiful. *God, keep us safe. This is crazy. How am I still alive? And Ken...*

Curtis put on his low beams as he took a right turn down a one-way street.

"You can smell the stench of death through the car." Eline tried to cover her nose and looked up at the pair of dark-skinned men in front of her.

"First time around dead bodies Eline?" Daren looked back at her.

"I've been around death, but it was livestock on the farm. A line of dead bodies on a back alley is something out of a movie or novel. It's foreign to me and my mind can't comprehend it."

Curtis drove down the one way slowly. "I forgot this engine was loud… should have gotten the four cylinder." Curtis maneuvered around a large truck.

Smack!

"Oh my God!" Eline shrieked.

A twitcher jumped on top of the window and started slamming its head into the glass violently.

"Go! Go!" Daren yelled.

"Don't worry, the glass is bulletproof. That thing can't break it, but I would rather not have that thing messing with my window." Curtis slammed the gas as the noise burbled from the back side of the ride.

"That exhaust is too loud, we're going to catch all of those things' attention," Daren said, looking frantic.

"I know man but you gotta go hard right." Curtis turned to the right as the crazed human flipped off the car. "Take this you damn thing!" Curtis put the SUV in reverse and slammed his rear bumper into the husk of the man taking its head off.

Curtis looked down at his rear camera and backed up again for good measure.

Eline breathed deeply. "I'm surprised more of those things didn't come out. You have a loud exhaust, Curtis."

"In our country, bigger is better and at the time I wasn't worried about crazy humans trying to jump on my perfectly waxed ride." Curtis whipped his head to the right, then looked north. "Something doesn't seem right."

Daren looked around and then back at Eline who had a usual smile on her face.

"What's wrong, silly?" Eline leaned her head to the right looking at him with a soft smile. Daren looked to the right as he saw a small crack in the glass holding a bullet.

"Damn!" Curtis put his foot on the pedal as he sped forward away from the gun fire.

"I am thankful for that bulletproof glass," Daren said, trying to sound optimistic.

The buildings passed by at a rapid pace as more gun fire hit the windows.

Eline looked behind them to see six lights appear out of the darkness. "Guys we've got a problem."

"I can see that," Curtis said, taking a right as he felt the bumper get hit by one of the trunks that pursued them.

Daren held the handle on the top of the door as the SUV skidded. "This is bad man, we should turn back."

"Ain't got nowhere to go little man. We got to keep moving forward." Curtis took a left as he sped down the road and hit the back of a small car.

"You've got nowhere to go," a voice said amplified over a loudspeaker.

"Damn…" Curtis went to put the car in reverse.

"I wouldn't do that if I were you," the female voice said in a mocking tone.

Curtis looked out the rearview mirror.

"Go, Curtis push it," Daren bellowed.

"I can't do that y'all. That's a rocket launcher. One wrong move and we could be blown to bits."

"Don't do it playboy. You guys need to come out and drop your weapons. We aren't about killing our own, that is if you are our own. If you're from uptown you're dead as soon as you walk out that door."

Curtis gripped the steering wheel as he slammed the wheel to the left and turned hard into the right.

"You shouldn't have done that playboy." the voice said in a mean tone.

Curtis sped down the road.

"Whew!" Eline shrieked. "You said we shouldn't outrun that thing."

"I faced worse things in war so I took our chances." Curtis turned to the right and down another back street.

"Oh!" Daren reached into his backpack and turned on the radio. "Let's see if they are communicating." Daren turned the dial as nothing but static came in.

"Why didn't they shoot us?" Eline peaked forward in between Daren and Curtis.

"It could have been a prop, empty, or a bluff. I'm thinking they want this ride for themselves. I took their bluff thinking they wouldn't shoot."

"That was a huge bluff..." Daren said, looking at him with wide eyes.

"I'd rather not get captured either. Rather die trying than get got." Curtis turned to the right.

BOOM!

"Hold on!" Curtis turned to the right as the impact from the large truck turned the SUV sideways.

"Oh my God!" Eline screamed as the SUV flipped three times.

The SUV sat silent, the wheel still spinning.

Daren looked back at Eline and Curtis who were both knocked out. He heard voices but couldn't make out what they were saying. Daren felt his head get dizzy as he felt his consciousness fade.

Chapter 8

June 3rd 2015

Aegis City – Hideout

0800

"Sit them up." a male voice said in a squeaky voice.

"You got it baby." a female voice answered.

Daren looked up to see a man on a gold colored couch. He was standing up with a gold cane and a huge belt with the initials C.K. on it. In front of him were ten women in tight lingerie holding rifles.

What the heck is going on?! God where are you? This is crazy! Jesus!

Daren looked over to Curtis who was looking up at the man. Daren felt his hands bound behind his back.

Eline looked over at him trying not to cry. Her head was bruised but bandaged. "Daren are you okay?"

"Bitch! Who told you to speak." a woman in a white lacy teddy said, kicking Eline in the back.

"Hey!" Daren said, jumping to his feet.

In a moment's notice Daren felt his face slam into the carpet below him.

"Now, now that isn't how we should treat our guests," the man's high pitched voice scolded. "I don't want my carpets getting dirty."

Daren looked up at the man, he wasn't wearing a shirt, but had denim jeans, and a gold chain. His six pack abs glisten underneath the large lamps in the velvet covered room.

"Hey ill-informed man on the couch, women in your profession should be wearing heels and not flats." Eline tried to smirk but felt her face hit the ground again.

The man stood up and walked down with a lean holding his gold chain. "Now the only reason bitch girl and your little friend aren't dead is because of him." The man pointed his gold jeweled studded cane towards Curtis.

"Why don't you tell them who I am." the man said, leaning down towards Curtis.

Curtis looked up towards the man with a slight grin on his face. "Friends, this is the Coochie King. Most people call him C.K."

"Now why do they call me the Coochie King?" the man asked, twirling in a circle trying to be dramatic but nearly falling in the process.

"It's because you get all the hoes," Curtis said in a monotone voice rolling his eyes.

"That is right my buff black friend. So, I have a proposition. It includes maybe all of you living through the next day. Who is the leader of this merry little bunch?" the man asked, sauntering around the room.

Daren looked at Curtis wanting to head butt him fiercely. He knew that if he tried a bunch of lead would be headed his way. *There is no way out of this situation… I guess we'll have to play it cool and see what happens.*

"I am the leader of the group," Daren said.

King turned around with an excited look on his face. "You're telling me" He was laughing at the thought, "the mighty Curtis Chop is letting you lead him? Hahaha! Let me clear out my ears. You are the leader of this group?" King gestured at the group in mock horror and surprise.

"Yeah, Curtis is helping us to get to where we need to be." Daren looked at King with fire in his eyes.

"It looks like you want to tackle me… but to do so would incite your death. Ha ha I do love it when my prey thinks they can do whatever they want. It doesn't matter what you want to do now. You are never getting out of here. My hoes will make sure you stay in line. You don't know who the fuck you're messing with." Turning his full attention to Curtis the King shook his head. "Curtis, you lost your shaft my good friend. You let this chump guide you. What happened to the man who used to run the streets?"

"When you get older wisdom becomes your best friend." Curtis said, cutting King a piercing glare. "I have my own reasons for helping the little man out."

"So be it! I can argue with your convictions. I have my own as well." King walked up to Eline looking at her with an appraising glare. "You could be one of my hoes" He drooled. His eyes sliding to her chest. "Your bust is lacking and your butt is flat…. We would have to fatten you up a bit." He mused.

"Take your cane and shove it where your nuts are," Eline said, spitting toward King's feet.

"You are a feisty bitch, aren't you?" King said, raising his cane back.

"Don't you dare!" Daren looked over at King wanting to punch his lights out.

"You're lucky to be alive, young man," King said, looking at him.

One of the women in black lingerie holding a sawed-off shotgun looked at Daren with a particular interest.

"You know what? I was going to do something, but I need to keep my pimp hand strong. Maybe I can smack those cheeks later in my chambers."

"Stop it with the games," Curtis said, looking at King.

"Not one for games huh?" King stepped back up to his golden colored sofa. "So, my proposition, because I am *kind.* One of my drug houses was hit with one of those cursed individuals. Everyone there is dead. I'd rather not have my precious hoes get hurt going there so to minimize casualties you three are going to go there and clear it out for me."

"No!" Daren stood up again.

The woman behind Daren lifted up her gun to knock him out.

"Not yet my precious girl." King held up a staying hand. "Let the man speak his mind. Even in the midst of certain death he still has the gall to stand up to me." Reaching over he put an arm around the waist of a girl in a red teddy standing beside his couch. He pulled her down to sit with her back against him. "He is powerless before me and my hoes" he stated in a hard voice a hand caressing the girl in his arms.

"I am not going to clear your drug house. We aren't going to do it," Daren said, starting to take a step towards King.

"You're a fighter…I can see that…so I will let you guys think about it." King sat on the sofa, leaning over. "All of you great citizens of our fair city have until evening to figure out if you are going to accept my request."

"Let me guess, the alternative is death?" Curtis asked, wanting to run straight toward King and headbutt him in the jaw.

"Yeah, but for the girl she will be my personal sex slave and mistress."

"Yeah, I don't think so," Eline said disgusted.

"We will see," King said, smiling slightly. "Take them away."

The trio felt their face being covered by blind folds as they were taken away from the velvet covered room.

Several minutes later, Daren looked around the room as a shotgun was pointed in his face.

"You're glad our good king let you have a chance. It's not every day he gets to meet one of his heroes."

"Good to know," Curtis said.

The trio watched as the steel bar closed behind them.

"How are we going to eat or drink?" Eline looked around at the dark room with a few lights illuminating the dark hallway.

"No food, weapons, or anything. We have no idea where our gear is, and our phones are gone as well. This is a horrible situation." Daren laid on the floor, his hand still bound by the rope from earlier.

"I wish they would unite us so we can at least stretch…I am starting to lose circulation in my arms," Eline said, trying to stand.

"This doesn't look too good, but we have to go along with what they say." Curtis walked over to the cold stone wall and leaned back. "I rather not die today."

"No weapons, no food, and at the mercy of some guy who is a pimp or cult leader. I want to slap him in the face." Eline tried to pull apart her ropes to get free.

"We won't be any good if we thirst to death and we have no concept of time either." Daren looked back at Curtis who was closing his eyes as if in a meditation state. Daren stood and sat by Curtis.

"I am so sore" Eline said, walking gingerly toward Daren. "Is it okay if I lean on your lap, silly?"

Daren blushed slightly and nodded.

Eline sat beside Daren and leaned her head slowly down on his lap. "I don't want to die, guys. I don't want to die. I want to live and get out of this place. I pray that God does something to free us. We can't die in some drug house without our gear. No way to call for help. There is no help out there. I feel like I am going crazy."

Curtis let out a sigh… "Do you remember the war of 1992? You may have read it in history books."

Daren looked over at Curtis who was opening his eyes slowly. "You mean the war against Devona?"

"Yeah, they were a small state nearby where Eline is from."

"Yes, I've heard of them. " Eline snuggled a bit closer to Daren. They were bombing us. My parents told me they almost died in the bombing. Everyday someone was dying over rubbish.... foolish things."

"There were great atrocities happening in that area of the world at that time. I was in the Federation Forces on the second line going in."

"I heard that war was unnecessary," Daren says. "My parents told me it was corporate greed."

"They aint lying. They sent all the poor from the inner cities around the country to fight a war for some private company."

"Greed… that is why a lot of my parents' friends died." Eline looked up at Daren. Her eyes were glistening with tears as they flowed down her face. Learning these before unknown details hurt...

Daren looked down at her with a tender smile. "We aren't going to die here. God has much bigger plans for us than to die from a pimp."

Curtis continued his story, "When I was over there, I saw all sorts of things I won't go into. I don't think much of God, but my mom always prayed for me every day. One day I was walking around a corner in the small city clearing out these huts. I kicked in a door and a child was holding a grenade in her hand. Her parents made her kill them and the village chief promised they would all go to heaven if their eldest child killed me." Taking a breath he continued. "I spoke in her native tongue explaining that heaven would be wonderful, but she had a full life to live. The child couldn't have been more than seven years old. No one should have to bear that burden. The child was brainwashed. I should have died that day because many of my friends died in the same way. Something stopped me from shooting that girl when I kicked down the door. Maybe it was God, maybe it was my mom or both. The one thing I know is that God is always on time. That is what my mom always said."

"That is crazy, Curtis. I can't believe you had to go through and see things like that." Daren stated looking at him wide eyed.

"I rarely talk about it, "Curtis said, squaring up his shoulder. "I let the counselor hear most of it. Take it as you will. I've seen death more times than I can count. I don't talk to God but for some reason he kept me here through all of the stupid decisions."

"What happened after you came home?" Daren looked at Curtis with a face of awe and concern.

"I left the force and started the Too Live Crew. The rest is history as they say."

"Curtis, with all of that money you didn't make an underground shelter or something like that?"

"You know what little man, humans going crazy due to some sort of terrorist attack or virus wasn't on my checklist. You are being unreasonable. You're tired and sore. You need to learn to control your emotions."

Daren trembled and snapped. *Control my emotions? CONTROL MY EMOTIONS!?* "Look where we are! We are trapped! Where is God in all of this? I have yet to see him show up!" He growled tugging at his restraints. *'The Lord is close to the brokenhearted that verse that damned verse if God was with them then was he?! Ken died! They were heading where they needed to go and then this prick of a king came and got them!*

All was silent for a few beats as Daren felt his heart sink…the rage dying into despair. "…but we are still alive. My hands are bound, and we have nothing…nothing, no way to communicate with anyone. We are all but dead…we are going to be killed by big breasted women in tight clothes."

The silence filled the cell once more, Eline shifted herself to sit up more. "The way you say it makes it sound awesome in a way." Eline looked up with a smile. "We are still alive. We have each other. God has us. We'll get out somehow…" she locked eyes with him, "You should learn to loosen up, silly." Sticking her tongue out playfully at him.

Daren tried to calm himself but couldn't contain the emotions in him.

"Hey, look at me God is with us right… then who can be against us," Eline said tears started to stream down her cheeks.

Daren took a deep breath. *This is hard for all of us...*

"You know what, little man? That rage inside you will keep you alive. Never let the passion in your heart die out but learn to manifest into something that can propel you forward." Curtis closed his eyes again, his head meeting the cold stone wall.

"Hey! You guys need to drink something. You are under the King's care now. That means you are his property. He can do with you as he pleases."

"You know what? We don't—" Daren spoke in a harsh tone.

"We humble accept his hospitality," Curtis said looking up at the fair skin woman in tight clothes.

The woman laid three glasses of water with straws in them from her bag and put them inside the cage. Another woman walked up with a shotgun to her back and a plate with three bowls of soup.

"You all better be thankful that the king saw fit to feed you before going on your mission," the other woman said in pink stockings.

"We are thinking about it," Daren said, trying to sound calm.

"I think that is wise," the woman with the soup said.

A third woman walked up with a pair of keys and a knife in her right hand. "The king said you can eat and have freedom of movement. He wants to give you the best chance of survival. My friend here will blast you to bits if you try anything."

The trio nodded as they struggled to stand up without the use of their hands.

After several awkward and failed attempts the girl looking for all the world put out, grabbed the back of their shirts one by one tugging hard to help them to their feet.

"Now turn against the wall," the woman said, opening the door.

The trio turned against the wall as they felt their restraints cut. The door shut as the three women looked at them with disgust.

"I can believe the master wasted his food on them. We could have cooked rats for them instead of giving them hot soup."

"If they are going to die then might as well plump them up," the woman in pink stockings said.

The girls turned their heads and walked off away toward the end of the hallway. Their exit was announced by a large slam of the steel door.

"I'm not eating that." Daren leaned against the wall, arms crossed.

Eline skipped forward twirling as she sat down In front of the bowl. She folded her hands and said a soft prayer in grace. Then she picked up the spoon and leaned it towards her mouth.

"Don't do it!" Daren started to run to Eline.

Eline put the spoon in her mouth and turned around with a smile on her face. "What are these spices?" Eline cheeks flared up. "This is delicious."

Daren almost slipped as he looked at Eline with a puzzled look.

Curtis stood up and walked slowly. "I guess she truly has the faith to trust God. She ate food from the enemy."

"That's not wise it's stupid." grumbled Daren swinging his hands outward, expressing doubt.

Eline took a deep breath. "I'm trying to be patient with you Daren, but we have to make it someway. You heard them. They aren't to kill us. Why not try the food they are going to give us."

"She does have a point, little man." Curtis sat in front of the bowl and took a sip. "The food is pretty good. If this is going to be my last meal, then it's not too bad."

Daren looked at Eline, who had already turned around taking another bite of the soup. "You guys are crazy. We are sore and in a bind. I'm trying here but things aren't adding up."

"Come sit," Eline said. "Please. We are going to make it. Remember what God tells us to walk by faith."

Daren clinched his fist as he walked slowly to the soup in the blue bowl. *Well God I guess it's now or never.* Daren sat beside Eline who was sipping the soup happily. He took a small sip.

Curtis looked over at Daren who was still unsure about the soup. "Dig in man… if they wanted to kill us, they already would have." Curtis smacked Daren on the back.

Daren coughed as the soup slipped down the wrong tube. "You almost made me choke man." He looked over at Curtis with an unapproving glance.

"I timed it right where it would go down the wrong pipe." Curtis took another sip of the protein filled soup and drank some water.

Daren shot a glare at Curtis but sighed letting it go. "If we are going to do this we need to come up with a plan." Daren sipped the soup gingerly, smiling at its warmth. *It is quite good.*

"I know they aren't going to give us guns… they will probably give us blunt weapons or maybe a knife or two," Eline said.

"The same thing crossed my mind," Curtis said. "I'm big enough to punch a few of those things but we still need protection. Maybe we can scavenge for some tape or something to wrap our arms up."

"Maybe they will put us in riot gear," Daren said in a joking manner.

"That would be something. We would actually have helmets and shields. It would be more defensive than anything." Eline chomped down on a potato she found in the soup, savoring its flavor.

"Against all odds we have to survive this. What if they shoot us right after we clear this drug house?" Daren scratched his forehead.

"We could make a run for it," Curtis said.

"Would this King let his women go with us… I mean he doesn't want to put them in harm's way." Eline took another sip of water.

"I think he will send a few of those 'weapons' to keep tabs on us and they are going to have guns or protection of another sort."

"We need to find a way to get the guns from them then." Daren looked over to the left and the right at his two friends.

"You know, little man, you got a good mind on you. We need to be careful. In war you have to wait for the right time to strike. We always gave a signal. I'm thinking like something pertaining to your age. How old are you?"

"I am twenty-four." Daren said, putting up a two and a four on his left and right hand.

"Still using fingers I see…well, there is nothing wrong with that. Eline, how old are you?" Curtis glanced over at her with a slightly nod.

"I'm twenty-six going on twenty…many people think I am younger than I look."

"It could be the country water you are drinking over there. It's probably more pure than anything we have." Daren let out a light chuckle while elbowing Eline in the shoulder.

"That hurt, but it's okay," Eline said, taking a sip of water. "Never have I wanted to hurt someone so bad. I don't know who I want to slap first. The pimp or the hoes."

"Look at you using some slang," Curtis said. "King can be a weird dude. Oddly, he does help the community in some respects. I don't agree with the way he does it."

"What do you mean?" Daren asked.

"As you can see, he uses women in a negative way. The community center a few blocks from here was built by him using those women."

Eline looked up from her soup and stared at Curtis. "So, he got the women to go out and have relations. He used the money to build a community center."

"That's right but I only found out through a source who came to my store once every few months. You know… you hear things and then it comes to light."

"That is horrible… but the women see it as giving back or so I heard." Curtis slid his bowl forward finishing his meal.

"I still don't like the man," Daren said. "That squeaky voice of his sounds like a chew toy or something."

"You got that right," Eline said. "I bet I could take him. I want one minute with him to lay some blows. God can let me have that right."

Daren and Curtis shook their heads laughing slightly.

"Yeah I think God would be okay with that," Daren said, putting his hand on her knee.

Eline smiled, putting her hand on his rubbing it softly. "Daren, have you taken time to process what is going on with your cousin?"

Daren thought back to the horrible moment on the roof where his cousin walked out declaring he would kill the man who took out his comrade.

"Honestly, no I haven't even processed it yet. It's there in the back of my mind but it's not time yet for me to unpack that. I love my cousin, but he also made his choice."

Curtis let out a sigh as he crossed his arms. "Yes, we are a sum factor of our choices. It could be good or bad, but we have to live with them. Correct me if I am wrong but the good book also talks about that."

"You are correct," Eline said cheerfully. "God can forgive us, but we have to sit in the pits we make especially if it leads to bad life choices."

"I want a chance to talk with him. To hear him out. There has to be a reason why he is gang banging. He doesn't seem like the type." Daren laid on the ground, putting his hands behind his head.

"Rarely do those who seem like they are capable of such atrocities will surprise you. With my ex-wife I didn't think she would steal a great deal of my money. She was our accountant. She took almost everything and went with a man. She got in a wreck in a exotic car because one night her boyfriend got high and drove off a cliff in the countryside."

"Wow…that's heartbreaking." Eline finished her water, looking over at Curtis with a warm look.

"All we have is today. You know what little man you are going to be okay. I am a firm believer that if you seek those answers will be shown to you. Do you truly want to know the answers or are you better off not knowing?"

Daren sat for a moment, looking up at the dull ceiling. *Should I remember Michael the way he was, or do I seek those answers from God? Jesus says to let those who dwell in wickedness to the wrath of God. What would I do if I found him? I love him. He is like a big brother to me. There has to be a reason why….* That card he got popped into his mind's eye again. *'The Lord is close to the brokenhearted' That has nothing to do with this!*

"If and when I see my cousin, I will have to decide the path that will lead me to the most peace." Daren looked at Eline and Curtis with a smile. "I am thankful that we are in this together." Taking Eline's hand Daren mused about how quickly she was becoming important to him. *Maybe I could see a possible future after this with her...*

Chapter 9

June 3rd, 2015

Aegis City – King's Hideout

1700

Smack! Smack!

The metal bars rang out in a sharp, loud tone as the trio woke up to see the women standing in front of them holding the same weaponry from before.

"King wants to speak with one of you. He said to bring Curtis."

Curtis nodded looking over at Eline and Daren.

The trio turned around putting their hands on the wall.

The woman in a black skimpy attire opened the door. "Now walk out slowly," the woman commanded.

Curtis turned around and walked slowly out the door. "No blindfold," Curtis said.

You're probably not going to see this place again, so it doesn't matter, the woman replied in a gruff tone.

Curtis walked forward towards the large steel door. Two women were in front and one behind him. He could take the one in the back, but then he would be blown away. It's best to keep moving. Curtis went through the door and walked down a carpeted hallway with large statues of King himself holding women in various poses.

Curtis followed the woman back towards the main lobby where Curtis was sitting on his sofa.

"Oh, nice to see you again, rap master Chop. Has your merry band of friends decided if they are going to help me?" King took a bite of a grape from his favorite woman. He looked at Curtis and licked his lips slowly.

"Your mannerism could use some work, King." Curtis crossed his arms.

"Because you make music, and we are the same shade of brown doesn't mean I won't put a bullet in you myself. The bigger they are the harder they fall right. I won't take any lip." King pointed at a woman in a light blue outfit.

Curtis felt the cold steel on the back of his neck. "Blowing my brains out means you have to sacrifice one more of your hoes, right?"

King licked his lip as he sat up from the sofa. "You are wise, apparently. Yes, my resources are spread thin because of this situation. If this was normal, I would have killed you already. So, what will it be?"

Curtis uncrossed his arms, his large muscles pulsating slightly. "We have decided that we would rather not die. We will go along with your game."

"That mouth of yours is quite salty." King leaned forward looking at Curtis with a disgusted glance.

"Why don't you come take care of it." Curtis rolled his shoulders slightly smiling at King.

"I'd rather not soil my hands with petty work. My girls will assemble the gear for you and fill you in on the details. Until then, pray or do whatever. I want one of my streams of income back. Thank you for cooperating." King laid back down on the sofa sipping a glass of wine.

Curtis felt the steel on the back of his head removed as he turned around guided by the women back to his cell.

Daren and Eline looked at Curtis and he walked in with a smile on his face. The cell closed behind him as the women walked off toward the entrance.

"You won't believe what this fool has in his I guess whore house is what I call it."

"Is it pictures of all his women doing unforbidden acts," Eline said.

"That is expected but no, he has paintings and status of himself. I mean like expensive…something you would see in a movie." Curtis sat down, facing the wall.

"Well after that sofa we saw, it could only get worse right?" Daren drank what was left of his water and he leaned against the steel bars.

"I hate the smell down here. It's musty," Eline said.

"I agree," Daren says. "Did you get any information on what's happening?"

"Yeah, we are going to be given some sort of gear to survive. As both of you know it's probably going to be the minimum amount of gear available. At least we are going to get something. I did however lay into him a little bit for you little man."

"Thank you for that," Daren said, smiling at him.

"Your concerns are valid. I wanted to let you know even though it's hard you have to keep it in and use it at the right time. For my comments, I got cold steel to my head. It reminded me of my days as when I was captured in the war."

"You were captured?" Eline asked. Her eyes widened looking at Curtis in awe.

Curtis looked over to Eline about to open his mouth.

"Hey! The King has given you the gear you need, a woman bellowed. We will let you get ready. We leave in fifteen minutes. You will have three of us go with you."

A dark-skinned woman who was bald walked forward. "I'm Sherri. I don't take no shit from anyone. You go one step to the left, I *will* blow your back out. As long as our resources are secure it doesn't matter what happens to you."

Another woman was holding a large bag. Her hair was blonde and in a bun, her frame was short, and she was quite plump around the thighs. Her smile was sweet but solemn.

"My name is Maria," she said in a soft voice. "King told us to prepare you for this. I'm here to go with you to ensure our resources are secured." Maria's brown eyes held a certain glimmer to them.

"My name is Victoria. I am our master's favorite." The muscular woman pointed her finger at herself. "I am the leader of this group." The woman wore a black leather jacket. On her back was a sawed off shotgun and her hip held what looked like a large revolver. "You guys have ten minutes to get ready. Now hustle."

Sherri opened the gate as the trio of women put their book bags down and headed towards the large steel door towards the entrance of the hallway.

Eline let go a slight giggle. "I thought they were going to fight in their undergarments."

"I'm surprised as well," Curtis said, opening his backpack.

"Anything useful in there?" Daren scoffed.

"Not much!" Curtis pulled out a small knife and some tape.

Eline pulled out some elbow and knee pads. "I feel like I am going to play hockey."

"This is like a butter knife." Curtis jeered, looking at his two comrades.

"What do they expect us to do with this?" Daren grunted.

"Probably die." Eline bellowed, looking at the bottom of the backpack. She pulled out four bottles of water and some snacks.

"What good is food if we have no weapons?" Daren pulled out an apple and two oranges.

"I wonder how far we have to go." Curtis stood, putting on his backpack. Curtis walked toward the bars, jiggling the slightly loose metal. He lifted up slightly.

The steel door down the hallway opened back up as a single woman walked down the hallway.

"Did you get it unlocked?" the woman asked, carrying a shotgun. Maria walked back, her eyes open wide. "You don't have much time."

"What?" Curtis asked, looking at her.

"I loosened up the bolts while you were all asleep. You are being sent to your death. I got captured. I am being held against my will."

"What if this is a trap?" Daren asked, looking at her suspiciously.

"Do you want to go to your death clearing some crack house?" Maria put her hands out jestering wildly.

"I think she is telling the truth," Eline said, smiling.

Maria smiled as she went to the bar where Curtis stood. She gently put her hand on his hand. "Lift up with me."

Curtis let go a slight smile as he lifted with Maria. Curtis lifted the bars as he put it to the side of the wall.

"Why are you helping us?" Daren hesitated.

"I want to get out of here. That man is a wimp and a sex maniac. I am being tortured by him. The way he treats these women they all worship him. We don't have time, we have to go now. There is a changeover in personnel where there is a five-minute gap at the end of this hallway."

Curtis looked over at Daren and Eline. "I don't trust you," Curtis said, "but your actions tell another story."

"What about this? Maria put down the large pack holding three pistols and holsters. "I was able to get a crossbow with three arrows."

Eline eyes perked looking at the crossbow. "This isn't mine, but it will do."

Daren picked up a revolver and put it on the belt.

Curtis picked up two pistols. "We could kill you right now."

"You wouldn't have a guide, would you?" Maria asked, looking around and panicking slightly.

"Come out this way." Maria turned around walking down the hallway.

Eline walked out first running after Maria who was already out of ear shot.

"I think she is serious," Daren said looking at Curtis who quickly followed Eline out of their caged prison.

"Come on, this way," Maria said quietly as she opened a door with a ladder going down.

"I'll go first." Maria went down the ladder and landed in the sewer water below. "Come on in the water is fine."

"That smell is atrocious," Daren said, plugging his nose. Gripping the ladder, he went down in the shallow water.

Curtis and Eline followed as the four of them looked at the large hole in front of them.

"The changeover should be happening any minute." Maria walked forward on the outskirts of the large oval entrance down a mouse infested waterway. She turned her flashlight down to the lowest level so as to not alter anyone to their presence.

"If this King was truly a king you would think he would hire an extermination service." Eline gasped as a dozen mice ran past the group of four.

"How do you know his area so well?" Daren spoke walking up towards. "I still think you could be leading us to a trap or making us feel hopeful to crash our spirits."

"We could still shoot her." Curtis proclaimed, trailing behind Daren and Maria.

"If you must know," Maria quipped "This is where King sends the girls he doesn't like. That would include me because I was a teacher before this. My previous boyfriend had a debt to pay, and he used me to pay it off. I was a fool. I was desperate for love and he had it all."

"Men can be a drag, can't they?" Eline bantered, looking up at Maria.

"Thanks," Maria said as she put up her hand. "Look ahead of us."

Before the group of four was a large four way intersection and a long hallway leading forward. It had the numbers 19, 34, 18, and 35 on the walls marking different paths.

"No one is there," Curtis whispered.

"Let me check," Maria whispered, walking forward.

Maria walked towards the large intersection as she checked both directions.

"You think she is still against us?" Elina asked, touching Daren's shoulder.

"It's hard to tell. In the current state of the city, it's hard to know who to trust. It feels like a movie," Daren assured her with a smile. "If she wanted to kill us she could have shot when she opened the door."

"Y'all look." Curtis pointed at Maria who was waving her hand.

The trio moved forward towards the 34 path. They walked past Maria who was keeping watch.

"You're not supposed to be here," a woman's voice came from the west 18 intersection.

"Shoot!" Maria exclaimed underneath her breath.

The woman walked up wearing a tight black bra and long black pants.

"Well, you see the thing is I am escorting them and the others see..." Maria put her gun and pointed at the woman's chest.

BOOM!

The woman swayed to the left and the right, falling to the ground in the pool of blood.

"RUN!" Maria yelled coming up behind Eline who was in stride.

"Oh shit," Curtis said, running forward splashing the water up to his ankles.

"I never liked her," Maria yelled, gasping for air. "Oh my God, I shot someone. I'm going to hell. I feel like throwing up."

"You would have to kill someone eventually," Daren said.

The group of four heard something coming from a distance.

"That's Victoria… we need to keep moving," Maria bellowed, turning the corner. "There is a cut through where the King transports his drugs through an old cathedral. It should be around the corner."

The water was growing in depth as Maria pointed with her flashlight a ladder in the distance.

"I see it," Eline said as she brought up the rear behind Daren.

"It wasn't this deep two weeks ago." Maria dove in, swimming forward grabbing the ladder in front of them.

Boom! Boom!

Bullets ricochet off the metal pipes.

Maria reached the top of the ladder soaked as she pushed aside a wooden plank. "Hurry!" she screamed.

Curtis gripped the ladder as he pushed his large frame up and through the opening.

"Come on Eline, let's keep it moving." Daren pulled out his pistol as he shot two bullets into the coming light down the tunnel.

"Come on little man! Come on!" Curtis panted helping Daren up through the crack.

"We are almost home free." Maria trembled looking around the small room for any towels to wipe the stench off their bodies.

Daren put his back down and looked down at Eline. "You're almost there!"

Boom! Boom!

Eline's face winced in pain and blood began to pour from her back.

"ELINE!" Daren shrilled, grabbing her wrists. *No No No No NO NO! I'm not letting her go!*

"It's okay silly," she strained to say, "you can let me go." looking up at Daren. Her eyes slowly swelled up. "I can feel my body going cold…. God has you…don't forget..."

"NO! We can get you somewhere or someone who can help you." Daren tightened his grip, trying to pull Eline up.

"I love you Daren…" Eline twisted her wrist with what strength she had left as her body descended into the water below.

Splash! The water enveloped her body, the blood emerging from her back like butterfly wings into the putrid water below….

"ELINE!" Daren tried to jump down towards her.

"Little man!" Curtis grabbed Daren and pulled him back up.

Daren turned towards Curtis and swung his fist with all his might into his shoulder.

"She's gone, little man. She's gone… Even if we got her out of there she would have died in your arms."

"Better to die in my arms rather than in a sewer." Daren kneeled on the dirty ground, the dim light in the room illuming the warm tears streaming down his face.

God why couldn't it have been me?

Shouts from down in the sewers could be heard. It seemed that the hoes below were having trouble getting up the ladder with the water and Eline's form blocking their path. "Get it out of my way!"

"We need to go… NOW" Curtis snapped, grabbing Daren and halling him up from where he had dropped to his knees.

Daren didn't care. He didn't even really hear what was happening around him anymore. His mind replayed her eyes, her resigned smile that had somehow been cheerful even in death… *The Lord is close to the brokenhearted… If so, where was God now? Why did he let her die? Why didn't he take him instead? Eline...*

To be continued in book 2

1 He said to them, "Go into all the world and preach the gospel to all creation. Mark 16:15

2 A thousand may fall at your side, ten thousand at your right hand, but it will not come near you. Psalms 91:7

3 Do not grieve, for the joy of the Lord is your strength. Nehemiah 8:10

www.ingramcontent.com/pod-product-compliance
Lightning Source LLC
LaVergne TN
LVHW090959080826
845145LV00003B/1058

* 9 7 8 1 7 3 5 8 3 9 4 2 4 *